THE SMUGGLERS' TALES

Denis Applebee

Matt 28:20

ARTHUR H. STOCKWELL LTD
Torrs Park   Ilfracombe   Devon
Established 1898
www.ahstockwell.co.uk

British Library Cataloguing-in-Publication Data.
A catalogue record for this book is available
from the British Library.

These are entirely fictional stories,
and no conscious attempt has been made
to accurately record or recreate
any real-life events.

ISBN 978-0-7223-4017-2
Printed in Great Britain by
Arthur H. Stockwell Ltd
Torrs Park   Ilfracombe
Devon

CONTENTS

PREFACE

When a father is left alone to put his children to bed, anything might happen. And anything did happen. The father had to devise a way to persuade those children that they just had to be in bed by the time their mother arrived home, or there would be trouble. What better way to blackmail a father than for his children to demand that if they went to bed, he must tell them a story!

That is how this story came to be told. Each Tuesday evening another chapter would unravel its mystery or humour. Sometimes Mother would come home too soon and the chapter ended rather abruptly. Sometimes she crept up on us and listened outside the door.

If at any time the reader does not find the excitement he expects, then it is because he does not have before him wide-eyed expectant children waiting for the moment of defeat or ridicule which gives the story its savour. If at any time the story takes on an adult atmosphere and language, then it is because the adult telling the story was at that moment living, in his own imagination, the happenings of that moment. Who hasn't wanted to leave the world of reality and enjoy a moment of excitement in the fantasy world of the smuggler or the highwayman of yesteryear? Well, here for a moment you can prowl through the night or ride the high tide in an open boat, always just eluding the King's men – always, that is, until . . . Well, read for yourself, and I hope you may even have some wide-eyed children to listen while you live out something of the life of *The Honest Smuggler*.

The smugglers rendezvous with the *Sea Winkle*.

THE HONEST SMUGGLER

To
Grace and Jonathan,
whose
excited listening made
the story.

CHAPTER ONE

A Matter of Conscience

The exact period and stage of my story does not really concern my reader, for smuggling has always gone on, and the South-West of England has so many smuggling havens along its rugged shoreline. This story could be set at any time during the sailing-ship era and at any place along that coast. I do not wish to incriminate either year, village or decade in the tale I have to tell.

What I must tell, however, is the reason for this act of smuggling, for I think it is unique in the annals of the 'trade'. In the first place, the leader of this smuggling band was not only a clergyman, but an extremely honest one. Had he not been so outspoken in his distrust of the taxmen of his day, and had he not been known for his upright living, the tight corners and traps set might have been avoided. But the fact of the case is he was an extremely honest man.

The government of the day was keen, as most governments of any day are, to collect as many taxes as it could. As long as those taxes were collected, it troubled itself little as to whether a little extortion took place in faraway areas of its jurisdiction. Lower Penzle was about as far away from the halls of power as you can get without dropping into the sea, and the market town of Crendon Bywater was the seat of local government. Crendon Hall was the seat of the seemingly all-powerful lord of the manor, Sir Richard Crendon.

Every penny collected in taxes flowed through his treasury before it finally got into the coffers of the King, and not a little seemed to get stuck to his fingers on its way! This 'little extra' was levied on everything brought by sea to the busy little port. No overland exclusions were allowed, and a very strong hand was kept on all routes into the marketplace, lest any should try to avoid such taxes as Sir Richard thought good for the community to pay.

This unjust situation came to the notice of the worthy young Rector of Lower Penzle. He was a man well read in the law of the land and well acquainted with tax revenues; for his own father, who had been dead for some six years now, had himself been an officer of the Crown, strong in principles, not only of loyalty, but justice. The Reverend John Trevethin shuddered as he surveyed his bill for several yards of cloth, purchased to adorn the windows of the rectory. How could there be so much tax on such a bill?

When the facts were made plain to him by the local shopkeeper, he breathed in through his front teeth and whispered under his breath, "We do not have to pay such rates, and neither shall we if I have my way in this living."

That is just where our story begins. He was declaring war on unjust taxes claimed by the lord of the manor. His was a war on dishonesty and extortion, which was making honest people desire to find a way round the law. Into this arena of local warfare stepped as brave a 'general' as ever commanded an army. If John Trevethin had been alive at the time of the Crusades, I suppose he would have ridden off to the East. As it was, he hardly ever rode outside his parish boundaries. Yet, wage a crusade he did, and successfully although the 'enemy' made continual counterattacks, as shall be seen as our tale progresses.

His crusade began, verbally, just four Sundays after his arrival at St Matthew's Parish Church as Rector of Lower

Penzle. The sermon included a rather powerful attack on unjust taxes, and it made Zaccheus look saintly alongside those responsible in Crendon Hall. In quick succession following that morning service, two things happened which John Trevethin was not expecting nor prepared for. The parish clerk called an extraordinary parish meeting and a lone horseman, Paul Slocum, was seen to ride off, missing his Sunday dinner to get the news of the sermon to Sir Richard at Crendon Hall.

The parish of Lower Penzle had been the hardest hit of any by the stringent tax collections. Its little harbour had, until Richard Crendon's rule, been busy with imports as ships called in on their way to ports higher up the coast; but now the inhabitants had to travel to Crendon Bywater, and, what hurt them more, they had to pay the higher taxes. That Sunday-morning sermon stirred more than religious emotions. Parishioners had long been discussing ways around the injustice of their situation. Now they had an ally in the most unexpected place: Lower Penzle's parish pulpit! The staid Anglican congregation sounded as if fervent Methodism had set it on fire. Of the parish meeting I will say more later. I must now follow that lone horseman out of the village and across the moors to a clattering halt in the courtyard of Crendon Hall.

Sir Richard was, strangely enough, entertaining his own parish minister when the rider was admitted. Sunday dinner was half devoured and the horseman's mouth was watering at the savoury smell of roast duck and minted potatoes as he asked permission to see Sir Richard alone.

His story was soon told. Sir Richard then bade his visitor follow him to his study, where he wrote a hurried note for delivery to the Rector of Lower Penzle. No sermon had caused such interest in many a year, and no sermon had gained such a speedy response. Sir Richard's letter was right to the point:

To the Rector of Lower Penzle.

Dear Sir,

Word of your most interesting sermon subject has reached me this noon hour, and I hasten to congratulate you on such an original theme. However, I would remind you that when I recommended your name to the Bishop, it was not that you should become a political busybody in the community.

If, sir, I should hear of further comments on the serious business of the King's revenue from your pulpit, I shall see to it that your living is removed from my patronage and you are removed from the diocese. Such matters as you have intruded upon are for those of us who are appointed to the same by the King. You, sir, profess – do you not? – to be appointed to higher matters by the King of Kings. Kindly reserve your enthusiasm for the realm of His domain and leave the mundane matters of this realm to those of us who carry the King's seal and authority.

I do not expect to hear or see anything of you in the near future. Efficient pumps work in silence!

Signed:

Crendon of Crendon Hall.

PS: This note is being delivered by one of your parishioners who happened to be visiting me today. I expect no reply but your unreserved compliance with my wishes.

CHAPTER TWO

The Underground Passage

When the first shock of reading had passed, the Reverend John Trevethin placed the letter on his study desk and felt the kind of thrill which comes from confrontation. He had no idea just how thrilling events were to become for him and those others who were this very night to begin the adventure of their lives.

Mrs Jones, John Trevethin's sturdy Welsh housekeeper, ushered the chairman of the parish council into the room.

"Will you have tea served now, or shall I wait for the others to come, rector?"

"You can bring the tea in and serve them as they arrive, Mrs Jones, thank you."

The rector was getting to know his housekeeper a little more, and Mrs Jones was becoming a second mother to him. But she was to be more than that, for with her sister, the wife of the local innkeeper, she was to become a useful source of information.

"Come in, Joseph, and sit in that chair; you'll be warm and will be able to hear better."

Joseph Trenbeath was a friendly type of man to have in charge of affairs. This John had found from his first day in the parish. He was to prove his worth to be that of pure gold. Whilst Joseph could not join in the amazing exploits of the smugglers, he was their greatest encourager.

One by one the men filed into the study; none said very much by way of greeting. All seemed to feel that something was in the air.

The chairman addressed the rector direct: "Mr Trevethin, sir, about that sermon this morning—"

Several coughs showed either that an epidemic had suddenly hit the men of the village, or that all were clearing their throats for a speech. John Trevethin listened as Joseph Trenbeath spelt out what all were feeling. The subject of the unjust taxation could not be left as the text of a sermon.

"Didn't you yourself say we should be doers of the word and not hearers only?"

This was the rector's cue to read Sir Richard's letter, and that brought a storm of protest. Each man grunted fit to cause Mrs Jones to think all the pigs from Prendegast's farm were in the study.

"My dear men," said John, "I am a law-abiding citizen, but if I knew of a way to get round the injustice of these taxes, I think I would do something about it."

And so it was that the Reverend John Trevethin became the head of a smuggling gang such as England had never seen. Every man amongst them was in every other respect a law-abiding citizen of the realm, and what they were about to do would take some explaining to their wives, but that night all twelve of them put their hands to the rector's in a pledge of loyalty and industry to thwart Sir Richard Crendon and his taxes. None could see ahead to the narrow escapes and near brushes with Sir Richard's men, but all were to grow in a brotherhood of cunning and good humour.

Joseph was last to leave that night, and, before he did, he amazed the young rector by revealing a secret that until then only he knew. Each man had left with a handshake and John and Joseph were left alone. Mrs Jones was putting on her shawl to accompany Joseph home down the hill. She was spending the night with her sister in a room she always kept at the inn.

"Rector," said Joseph, getting up from his fireside chair, "just have a look at these bookshelves, will you?"

Together they ran their hands over the fine mahogany. On each shelf were some of John's finest volumes, but what John had not noticed as he had stacked his books was a latch carefully disguised under the third shelf. As Joseph placed his index finger under it and pulled forward there was a click, and then John almost lost his balance. The bookshelves moved out towards them both. The hinge was so carefully concealed that it was almost invisible. There before them both was a black opening in the wall.

John recovered from his amazement enough to take the lamp from the fireplace and illuminate the opening. Steps led away downwards in a tight-twisting stairway. Where to, he hadn't the faintest idea. The cellar? Another exit from the house?

They both looked down the little way made visible by the light to where the steps turned out of sight. Joseph quickly pushed on the door, and the shelves went back to their place as Mrs Jones tapped on the door to say she was ready to leave if Joseph was.

CHAPTER THREE

The First Meeting

Just how Sir Richard Crendon heard of the pact, or how much he heard of it, no one would ever know, but when the rector and his men met to discuss plans for the first attempt at smuggling goods past the taxmen they were already aware that their task would not be an easy one. The Reverend John Trevethin had fully investigated the winding stairway from behind his study bookcase down under the cellar of the old rectory. Part of the tunnel downhill had collapsed and needed much work doing on it. But after a few days digging by Matthew LeMas, the local gravedigger, working from the other end of the tunnel through the foundation and crypt of the church, it was possible to walk fairly easily from the rectory to the church without a soul knowing anyone had left the house.

Before the tunnel was shown to anyone else, a good deal of talking went on to make absolutely sure each member of the parish council would at all times preserve the secrecy of all that was to be divulged. The eyes of all concerned nearly popped out like organ stops when John revealed the secret. This was to be their regular exit from the rectory, and sometimes it would be the only safe way back. Everyone wanted to know its history, and the parish chairman was quick to tell the story, though it all happened long before any of them were born.

"In 1685", began old Joseph, as if he had actually been there at the time, "the Lord Chief Justice of England was the notorious George Jeffreys of Wem in Cheshire. He was busily engaged in the Bloody Assizes, following the years of Cromwell's Commonwealth. So many men were in danger hereabouts that the good rector of the parish had this tunnel secretly dug – strange to say, by the then gravedigger. Many a priest escaped with his life along its dark path and lived to tell the tale. My grandfather knew much more than I can recall, and he shared the secret with me. I was on oath that I would never let it be known unless it was to save life. Oh, I have wanted to tell the story a hundred times, and tradition would have had me share it with my grandson before I died; but here we are, and I don't think I have betrayed my trust."

To this they all said a hearty amen! They all smiled as the rector asked whether such a use of an amen was warranted, but the laugh in his voice made them all feel the warmth of their common trust, and they got down to planning the first meeting with a ship out in the bay.

Ben Grundle knew one of the two captains who plied their trade around the coast and felt he could trust him to share the secret. He could be contacted any time the ship was in port at Crendon Bywater, and such an arrangement was planned for the very next week.

This first meeting went well, except that on the way home they were overtaken by none other than Paul Slocum, who had first borne that critical sermon to Crendon Hall.

"Hi there, my man! I've seen you often in church, but never spoken yet."

The rector knew only that this was the man who had handed in the letter from Sir Richard late on that Sunday afternoon. Even Mrs Jones didn't take the trouble to name him then.

"I'll have you know, rector, that I'm not your man, as you say. I'm a law-abiding citizen and want nothing to do with fighting against the King."

"And what might you mean by that, Mr— I don't think I

even know your good name," continued the rector, while the rest of his little party rode on in silence and waited a little way ahead.

"My good name is Paul Slocum, rector, and I want that name to be kept good. I have been in the service of Sir Richard Crendon, and I did not like your insinuations. I will not sit in church to hear such. When sermons come from the Bible rather than being merely your critical ideas about those who're only doing their duty to the King, I'll be back in church. Until then, you can count me as a good Methodist – though m'father will turn in his grave to hear of m'descent!"

Here, then, was a man to be respected – not for his views or his loyalty to the Throne, but for the danger he might pose to the smugglers. Paul Slocum must be watched, and where he was must be noted before any excursion could be made from the harbour out into the bay.

The smugglers awaited with excitement their first attempt, and many a wife was curious to know why her husband spent more time than usual down at the harbour, or out in the bay fishing – more often than not, bringing home precious little to show for the effort.

The night came and everything went according to plan as they assembled first for a parish-council meeting and then for a trial run along the tunnel and through the graveyard to the harbour. Then they slipped their moorings and sailed quietly out to the open sea. They met the ship as planned, but, also as planned, nothing was unloaded this time. Every chance of being caught must be allowed for and every member of the crew checked if the plan was to work. Nothing went wrong. The small boat slipped back to its place at the foot of the steps, and no one else stirred along the quay whilst each man made for his home in the moonlight.

CHAPTER FOUR

A Spy on Hand

Following that first successful run-through of the planned smuggling, they did not have to wait long before the real thing. On the night chosen to meet a ship in the bay, there was no moon and distinct signs of rain in the air as the parish council met in the rector's study. Each man had brought a change of clothing and a lantern. Anyone watching them trudging up to the rectory might have noted sweat on some brows, for they wore more than enough clothing for such a night. But theirs was to be a night out on the water, and they knew not for how long, if the ship was late.

Little secrecy was used. It had been publicly announced that the rector desired to share a fishing trip with men of the parish, so there were one or two very curious faces lifted over the sea wall to watch them row quietly out of the harbour and make for the usual fishing ground a couple of miles offshore.

One vigilant witness was, as you might have guessed, Paul Slocum. He was of nosey temperament anyway, and this bit of unusual behaviour on the part of the rector did not miss his scrutiny. But before he lost sight of the small boat with its merry crew, it began to rain in the way it does on the Atlantic coast of South-West England – a fine drizzling rain, cutting visibility to almost nil. Whilst it made the going less pleasant on board the small rowing boat, it was welcomed as a very convenient screen. If the rector had not been a little touchy about the subject, someone might have hazarded a suggestion that God was smiling on their venture – but it was a wet smile if it was one at all.

Peter Simple was better than a compass on this murky night. It was as if he could see both shore and ship, for he handled the helm so well that they actually heard the voices of the seamen aboard the coaster before they saw her slowly come into sight. Six flashes on the rector's lantern were duly answered by seven from the ship. Quietly a line was thrown and caught. The small boat bumped against the heavy ship's side and the rector was given a hand and a pull on to its deck.

"Hi there, me hearty! So we've made it right on time," greeted Captain Storeton.

Before the rector could get his breath to answer, Captain Storeton was issuing orders.

"Look lively, Mr Poulton, sir, and get the goods up here."

A scuffle of feet took place with hardly a word spoken between the first mate and the crew as six kegs of spirits, four cases of tea, and a long, rather awkward roll of Flemish cloth were handed down to the men in the boat. With a brief farewell, the rector was lowered back into the boat and the line was cast off. It dropped with a splash into the tide as the coaster glided out of sight into the rain and darkness.

"If that is all there is to it, we are home and dry, gentlemen!" said the rector, almost whispering as if someone were listening to pass on the details to Sir Richard. "But I'm afraid that is not all there is to it. It was one thing to give a picture of a happy fishing trip on the way out, but it will be a very different thing to get these goods ashore unnoticed, even on such a night as this."

"All we need now is to find our friend Paul Slocum waiting for us," said Timothy Wiseman, the grocer of the village.

Sure enough, though it was three o'clock in the morning, there he was, standing behind the harbour light as they slipped into their moorings. Quick thinking on the part of the rector brought the man out of the shadows, startled enough to be off his guard.

"Hello there, Mr Slocum, sir. Kindly take hold of our line and we shall be much obliged." And then, to his crewmen: "Cover the stuff with your waterproofs and we'll send down for it later."

"But, sir," whispered Daniel Perry, the blacksmith, "how do we cover the cloth?"

Now, that was a question well asked, for here they were with a roll of cloth big enough to betray them all.

As Paul Slocum dutifully disappeared with the line to make it fast around a bollard on the other side of the harbour wall, the rector spoke quickly: "Grab that sail lying in Stephen Nye's boat there, and wrap it around the roll."

This was done in seconds, and the rector addressed himself again to Paul Slocum: "Mr Slocum, sir, I'm afraid we haven't much fish to offer you for your wait, but if you would assist us with this sail, which has to go up to Mrs Perry's for repair, we would all be obliged. Most of us don't go home that way, and I think you live not far beyond Daniel's forge."

As the man heaved and hauled to get the awkward sail up the steps from the boat and then carry it from the harbour to the village street, the rest of the company dared not even speak a word of thanks for fear they would laugh fit to burst their sides. Paul Slocum actually assisting in the very act of smuggling! Oh, that was too funny for words!

CHAPTER FIVE

The Officer of the Law

Paul Slocum paid his usual weekly visit to Crendon Hall, where, although retired, he still helped the new gardener, and, you may be sure, transported news of all that transpired at Lower Penzle to Sir Richard. Cap in hand he stood waiting for permission to speak. Sir Richard delighted in the little courtesies that had to be paid to him in his position and he looked at Slocum out of the corner of his eye as the poor man screwed his cap round and round in nervousness.

"Well, you've news of my learned friend the rector, I hear."

"Yes, sir, if you please, sir. He's been out fishing at some pretty strange hours, sir."

"Is there a law against nocturnal fishing?" rasped Sir Richard, enjoying the reddening face of Paul Slocum, as the poor man wondered if he really had anything to tell.

"Well, did you see anything strange about the boat or the men other than the time?"

"I noted that it was the same night as the *Sea Winkle* docked here, sir."

"Was it, now!" whispered Sir Richard to himself. "Now, that is very interesting, Slocum. You did very well to tell me. I think there is a pot of last year's pickled onions you may take home with you – and, mind you, watch the harbour until I can get someone official-like to step down to Lower Penzle."

With this, the conversation was over and Sir Richard was left alone to ponder the possibilities. Captain Storeton he never had liked. He was far too strict with the accounts of what was taxable and what was not; every tax collector knew how difficult it was to interpret the regulations and found it much easier to make a general levy on a cargo.

Sir Richard dipped his quill in the ink pot and scratched a letter to his brother, Josiah Crendon, forty miles away in Truro. This brother held a position of great influence over the King's men barracked in the town. He requested that an officer be dispatched to investigate suspicious circumstances relating to tax evasion in the neighbourhood of Crendon Hall.

So it was that some ten days later, on a cold Monday morning, a rather portly officer with a very red nose and bright, beady eyes stepped out of the Plymouth-bound coach in Crendon Bywater town square. A thin, long-nosed sergeant struggled with a large wooden trunk and a linen bag as the second coachman impatiently gave him half a hand on to the side of the road. The two soldiers, buttoned up to the collar as if it was midwinter, looked as ill assorted a pair as you could hope to find in the King's ranks. Coughing and puffing, the officer asked for Crendon Hall. A finger pointed up the hill amidst the trees, but the officer could see neither house nor road and he sat heavily on his trunk. The Sergeant attempted to do the same, but he was promptly pushed off its sloping lid and sat for a moment in a most undignified heap on the road – much to the amusement of the maids of the Coach and Horses Inn, looking through the windows.

"Get up, man, and scout around for some way we can get ourselves to Sir Richard Crendon."

The Sergeant dutifully rose, but tripped on the hem of his heavy topcoat as he did so. This time he fell backwards into the path of a passer-by.

"Look where you're sitting, man," said the stout newcomer. "Do you happen to be the officer who has come in answer to my letter?"

"I am the officer you refer to, sir," said a rather red-faced officer, rising to his feet with as much dignity as his heavy coat would allow, "and this is my sergeant. Stand straight, man!" said the officer in the same breath.

"Well, I might have suspected the man was drunk by his antics as I arrived, but I'll take your word that he isn't. Accompany me into the sitting room of the Coach and Horses. I am not accustomed to talking of my affairs in view of cackling maids and barking dogs, sir. This way!"

Sir Richard strode into the inn as the door was opened by a curtsying maid, and the officer followed, looking a trifle like an obedient, overgrown puppy. The Sergeant, who by this time had recovered his composure, attempted to follow the other two men through the doorway. Unfortunately for him, the maid did not see him coming and the door slammed shut, hitting the Sergeant full in the face. He went backwards like a tree falling in the forest and landed flat on his back. He caught a dog a glancing blow as he fell, and that mean animal took no pity on him, nor had any respect for his uniform. He yelped and took a savage bite at the spindly leg nearest to him. The Sergeant gave a cry of pain and charged through the door into the hall of the inn. The poor man had no time nor ability to avoid the innkeeper as he walked, tray in front of him, to the front sitting room. The tray upturned and hot ale drenched the publican's clean shirt. The Sergeant stood rigidly to attention, and it seemed as though all the inn came into the hallway to inspect the damage. A shout from the officer took the wretched individual out of earshot of the invectives which were flying as the innkeeper was lifted to his feet by every member of the staff at once.

The Sergeant stopped just inside the sitting room door and waited to be court-martialled. However, luckily for him, the commotion had not interrupted the conversation between the two men seated within, and Sir Richard stated to these two representatives of the King that he expected that they would not fail in dealing with the first serious threat Sir Richard had ever had to his rule of 'law' and order.

When the interview was over, the Sergeant was dispatched to find a cart suitable to transport the two men and their luggage to Lower Penzle.

"C-c-can't we stay here the night, sir?" said the poor man, almost a nervous wreck.

He certainly did not feel like a bumpy ride in the evening air before at least having a meal.

"We'll have a meal before we leave, but Sir Richard has kindly reserved us quarters at the White Horses in Lower Penzle."

"Oh dear, oh dear, oh dear!" moaned the Sergeant as he disappeared out of the door, looking very carefully to avoid the innkeeper or any other object he might send into disarray as he made his exit.

His task was not a difficult one, for he found a cart going to Lower Penzle in an hour's time, and the carter was only too willing to make it a paying journey. The two men, filled well with bread and cheese and hot ale, sat themselves on the cart. The officer occupied the box at the side of the driver, and the Sergeant was jammed, like a piece of toast in a rack, between the boxes and the officer's trunk in the back. He fell quickly into a fitful sleep, but the officer had the unenviable task of keeping up a conversation with Ben Pearson, who was as deaf as a post and had a voice fit to wake the dead. It seemed he believed the officer to be as deaf as he was, and the horse too, so all the way, some twelve miles up hill and down, the countryside rang with the shrill cries of old Ben as he kept up a one-way conversation.

CHAPTER SIX

A Duel at the Rectory

Mrs Jones had just completed her daily dusting in the rector's study when the bell rang almost off its hook in the hallway. Someone was in earnest about getting to see the rector, that was for sure. As the housekeeper opened the door, she only just prevented herself saying something rude to the puller of the bell. But the man who now stood with his back to her was in military uniform, and she coughed almost apologetically to turn him around. The rather small, round man who faced her when he did turn was not in the least military in his looks. That red face with bright, beady eyes might have belonged to a plump baby in a carriage.

Very much short of wind, the owner of the baby face announced in a breathless voice that he wished to see the rector. Standing a little way away from the front steps of the rector's front door was a second and taller man, also in military uniform. When both were ushered into the hallway, it was obvious to Mrs Jones that one was over-tall and one very much overweight, making an ill-assorted pair. Were they really military men, she wondered, or part of a wandering actors' troupe? The rector had similar thoughts as he came forward and invited both men into his study.

The smaller of the two cleared his throat in such a way that the rector could only think of his bishop about to make a long speech.

The officer began: "My dear rector, may I introduce myself? My name is Captain Willoughby Winton Williams of the 3rd King's Rifle Brigade; and this is my assistant, Sergeant Egbert Sigrose of the same regiment. We are here at the request of Sir Richard Crendon of Crendon Hall."

"Well, I'm pleased to make your acquaintance, Captain, and you, Sergeant."

"Oh, I'm very pleased to meet you, sir – very pleased indeed," gabbled the surprised sergeant, not used to being included in any introduction or welcoming ceremony such as this.

The Captain broke into his reverie and caught up the thread of his introduction again.

"I said I was here, rector, at the request of Sir Richard Crendon of Crendon Hall, and you may know that this esteemed gentleman is the King's representative in all matters of tax collection."

"If you mean, do I know that Sir Richard collects more than his required taxes, the answer is yes, I know it all too well. I would be obliged if you could do something about the discrepancies we all suffer."

The officer coughed as if he would burst a blood vessel and cleared his throat yet again.

"I am not here to discuss with you the merits of Sir Richard, who I am sure is as loyal a servant of His Majesty as I am. I am here to inform you as a minister of religion that both my assistant and I shall be remaining in these parts for a considerable period to investigate any infringement of the law in respect of tax collection."

"I'm more than pleased to hear that, Captain," said the rector with almost a smile. "I will be pleased to give you all the information I have collected, in the few weeks I have been in this parish, regarding the unjust collection of taxes. Where would you like me to begin?"

The officer attempted to rise to his full height off the chair. Unfortunately, his greatcoat was a trifle long for his height, and he stood on it as he rose. It only allowed him to rise halfway to a standing position, so he quickly sat down again.

The rector rang the bell for Mrs Jones. The good lady appeared with steaming hot tea and hot buttered crumpets as if it were a quiet ladies' afternoon meeting with the rector.

The Captain cleared his throat yet again, but this time he was left speechless as his eyes caught sight of the butter dripping off the edge of the crumpet nearest to him.

"Oh, my dear rector, this is too good of you. I did not expect you to go to such trouble to entertain officers of the Crown. You must have known my favourite morning repast was hot buttered crumpets."

"He likes 'em at any time, Your Reverence," interjected the Sergeant, who reaped the just reward for such a comment when a sharp heel descended on his ankle bone. He let out a shriek that scared the rectory cat out of its basket.

The mood had been changed so dramatically by Mrs Jones' entrance that the rector did not pursue his line of conversation; the Captain certainly did not show any sign of spoiling his favourite repast. But the rector was by no means feeling as hospitable as the tea tray seemed to indicate.

"Oh, Mrs Jones," said the rector in a stage whisper, "I think the gentlemen were just about to leave when you came in. We must not distract the King's men from their duty."

This time the clearing of his throat sounded like a drowning man coming up for the last time as the Captain pictured those delicious hot buttered crumpets going back to the kitchen uneaten.

"Oh, I wouldn't dream of offending the dear lady by not accepting what the good soul has prepared for us, sir. I think I could reasonably excuse any man, even on the strictest time limits, if he graciously accepted such a lady's kindness."

The speech was too much even for the rector's hardening heart, and they all sat down to munch at the crumpets, the Captain tucking a large, white handkerchief into his collar as if he were there for a full evening dinner.

It was as if all three men had put away their swords when the King's men finally took their leave of the rector. But it was a truce, not the end of hostilities, that was very certain.

The two men, casting long and short shadows, marched away down the hill in the morning sunshine. They had much to talk about, and the rector went back into the house with much to think about. It was now obvious that there was suspicion in the air, and future tactics must be worked out with more than Paul Slocum in mind.

CHAPTER SEVEN

Midnight Vigils

Life in Lower Penzle went on much as usual for most of the next month, but Ben Grundle did have a meeting with Captain Storeton of the *Sea Winkle* at the Terrapin Inn in Crendon Bywater. However, no such meeting went unobserved by Sir Richard. Though plans were made to have a casual meeting of the parish council, the Captain got to know of it and posted himself and the Sergeant in the bushes of the rectory garden. It was not a comfortable position, and I am sure the Captain should have at least brought some food with him, for it was to prove a long and unsuccessful vigil.

What puzzled Captain W. W. Williams was that he was sure he counted twelve men going into the rectory and only eleven coming out. Was the rector in the habit of entertaining members of his parish council to a night's lodging as well as an evening's business? Neither his limbs nor his stomach would allow him to remain much beyond midnight, for the former would have cracked with squatting in such an unnatural position, and the latter would have set up such a rumbling that his whereabouts would have been detected by everyone coming through the rectory garden. But where, oh, where, was that twelfth man?

Peter Simple was that man. He had that night been dispatched through the tunnel to the church crypt for a piece of organ music. Not that this was a usual procedure or route to the church; the rector had asked him to go that way so that he could let them know if all was well in this secret passage. It was not. During the month since last they all trundled through it the tunnel had suffered another collapse. Peter Simple asked if he might go back and put matters right and then leave by the church exit and go home. The twelfth man, therefore, was just leaving the church as the Captain and his sergeant were coming down the hill from the rectory garden.

'Well, well!' thought the Captain. 'I wonder how he got here from the parish-council meeting this evening.'

'Well, well!' thought Peter Simple. 'What is the Captain doing out so late – and coming down Rectory Lane too? He hurried on, not wanting to be caught in a conversation. The Captain, likewise, held back, not wanting to have his late walk noted. But both had seen each other and noted the facts.

When the rector was informed of the Captain's presence at the rectory that night, he realised they could no longer work in the open. The next meeting must be either somewhere else or at a time when the Captain was otherwise engaged.

The night for the next sea trip had arrived. Captain Williams knew all too well that the *Sea Winkle* was due, so he was vigilantly watching and listening for every move in the village. No parish-council meeting had been arranged, so it was not likely that the men would meet at the rectory, but one could never tell what might be planned. In the hope of finding out more, the Sergeant was dispatched to sit among the bushes of the rectory garden.

His sitting there was noted by Mrs Jones first, and then his presence was confirmed by the rector, looking out of an upstairs window. The poor man looked so uncomfortable squatting there that the rector thought about offering him a chair! But the serious matter of warning all the conspirators not to come as planned was the rector's most pressing problem. He wondered if they could meet at the church. But Mrs Jones was dispatched to the White Horses to make it plain that no one was to come to the rectory that night.

Mrs Jones hurried up Rectory Lane just as fast as her legs would carry her, and she was out of breath when she finally sat in her comfortable kitchen chair and faced the rector with some surprising information. First, the Captain had taken sandwiches and a flask of hot soup for what he had described as an 'evening out'. Putting two and two together, that meant that he would be somewhere out in the village watching. What were they to do?

Jonathan Peirpoint also sent the strangest message with Mrs Jones that he, the local undertaker, was going to wait upon the rector with a number of new coffins later that evening and would be obliged if he would cast his eye over their design. Such a request the rector had never heard of. It was the deceased's relatives who chose a coffin; what had he to do with such matters? However, there it was. Jonathan and his helper for the evening, Timothy Wiseman, arrived at the rectory in the undertaker's covered hearse, and without further explanation they lifted the first coffin into the rectory hallway. The door was closed and the Sergeant, watching from the garden, was left wondering who had died in the rector's household. He had seen Mrs Jones and the cat, which had already investigated the stranger in the garden. Who could it be? He, however, was not as mystified as the rector himself at this seeming display of craftsmanship of a rather morbid kind. The rector's eyes nearly left their place and knocked his glasses off when Jonathan lowered the coffin to the ground and, after lifting the lid, assisted Stephen Nye from its silken comfort.

"Well, I'm blessed! Well, I'm blessed!" said the rector over and over again. And then all four men laughed to the point of bursting. Mrs Jones suggested that it was rather irreverent, and she said such affairs should have some dignity, but all Jonathan could say was that he hoped no one would now ask for a second-hand coffin at a cheaper price. The men hurried out to bring the four other coffins in for display. Each time they would carefully carry the previous one out, and the rector would say in a very loud voice that he was not at all sure whether anyone would want to pay for such shoddy workmanship. His crowning words nearly lost everyone their composure: "I wouldn't want to be seen dead in a thing with as little taste as that!"

Each coffin contained another member of the parish council, and each of them in turn was lifted carefully down from the wagon as if it were empty and carried into the rectory for inspection. It was hot work.

The conspirators settled in Mrs Jones' back kitchen for several cups of tea before slipping into the rector's darkened study and down into the tunnel. Jonathan, alone, made his way down the hill to put away his coffins for future use on more solemn occasions. Finally, the poor sergeant was to be seen easing himself out of his cramped position and trudging downhill. As he went, he mumbled to himself that the rector was a man hard to please – extremely particular about his future burial attire!

CHAPTER EIGHT

Moonlight Serenade

Down in the tunnel the men, with lowered heads, made their way to the crypt of the church. There was a stillness one would expect at that time of the night, yet all had the same question in their minds: where was the Captain? They knew that he had left the White Horses with a hot flask and some food, but where was he now? He might be sitting right above them meditating in the darkness of the sanctuary. He might be sitting on a tombstone in the graveyard. Someone would need to spy out the land. The rector made his way quietly up the winding stone steps and slowly opened the door into the choir vestry. He didn't have long to wait to learn the answer to their question. He heard grunts coming from the far end of the church. Slipping into the nave, the rector could just see, in the light from the moon, a silhouetted pair of bow legs laboriously climbing the ladder into the belfry.

A council of war was needed. The rector went below and discussed the matter with his men. Captain W. W. Williams was obviously going to keep a lookout from the church tower, and he would see everything across the whole sweep of the bay. Even an owl and a pussycat in a pea-green boat would be visible to this man's beady eyes from that vantage point.

"I've got an idea!" said Donald Creedy, the youngest of the parish men and an assistant at the draper's store in the centre of Lower Penzle. He was also the newest and quietest member of the parish council, and for that reason all listened as he spoke his mind. The more he said, the more the men had to restrain their laughter; for if they carried out his plan, the whole village would hear about it. No vote was needed to show that all agreed with him, and the rector sent him aloft with his blessing.

Up in the belfry the short-winded Captain Willoughby Winton Williams was breathing the night air like an asthmatical donkey trying to bray and not quite hitting the note. He carefully surveyed the huge church bells, each standing poised as though ready for a wedding to request their service.

"Now, that I must mind," said the Captain aloud. "It wouldn't do to wake the village from its slumber – no, not at all, it wouldn't." Below him, in the bell-ringer's chamber, young Donald Creedy heard him and wondered just which bell he was nearest to up there. The creak of a board gave his position, and Donald reached upward to the loose knot of bell rope and gave it just the slightest pull.

So swift was the sweep of the downward-plunging tenor that two bats in its throat had little time to abscond before they were deafened by the clang of the hammer. The Captain jumped a foot off the belfry floor and shouted aloud: "I didn't touch it; I didn't touch the thing; honest, I didn't!"

'Now what do I do?' he wondered. 'One thing for sure – I must get out of the church before someone comes to find out who's ringing the bells at this unearthly hour. Oh, I do hope no questions are asked at the inn or I'll be the first suspect.'

As he moved around the belfry to find his footing on the ladder, the vibration of that first bell set off the lighter ones, and a terrifying din shot through the night air, sending birds and bats scurrying out of the louvred windows of the bell tower. The Captain was beside himself. He hardly managed to keep his footing as he half slid from one step on the ladder to the one below. It seemed as though all the bells were now ringing. The night was alive with their merry sound, telling the whole village, "Come and see the Captain descending, all his new hose rending, as he catches up his coat, running with a drying throat!"

The Captain hurried out of the church porch, not even noticing Donald Creedy standing in the moonlit choir stalls, chuckling to himself in uncontrollable laughter.

Donald realised when he descended the stairs into the tunnel that the lanterns were out; the men had not waited to see if the ruse was successful. So he doubled back a shorter way to the inn. There he just left a suggestion in the minds of the maids, busy with their cleaning, that the Captain had been practising as a bell-ringer. They giggled, and were still at it when the Captain walked guiltily in at the back door.

"Oh, sir, weren't you afraid of waking everyone up, ringing them bells so late?"

The poor man coughed and spluttered something about being interested in bats in the belfry. He stumbled through to the staircase and up to his room as quickly as his feet would carry him.

Out in the bay, with bright moonlight to help them, the smugglers rowed their way out to the waiting *Sea Winkle*. It had been moored for half an hour awaiting some signal either from shore or boat. Now it came: six flashes of the lantern. The signal was answered by just one more. The meeting was complete, and laughter rang out as loud as the bells when the rector told the reason for their sounding across the bay at such an hour – a perfect moonlight serenade.

CHAPTER NINE

The Cheese Race

Following a night's smuggling there was always some difficulty in transferring the smuggled goods to the shore from the boat. To be caught red-handed by a waiting officer of the King would have been all too easy. Often the goods were left in the boat, or at least at the harbour, until another time.

One particular morning, Timothy Wiseman was responsible for finding a way of transporting the previous night's proceeds to their final destinations.

All morning both the Captain and the Sergeant had been about the village streets, and it was obvious to Timothy that he could not openly make the journey from the harbour to his shopfront without being seen.

"Mother," he said, addressing Mrs Wiseman in the shop, "get the boy to put three sacks of sugar and two large cheeses on the cart. I'll take them down to the harbour with me."

"Now, that's the first time I've heard of cheese bait for herrings," said she with a twinkle in her eye.

"You're wrong, Mother, my dear. It's a sprat to catch a mackerel this time!"

The cart went very slowly with its brake shoe under the rear wheel to keep it from pushing old Daisy, the grocer's mare. Down at the harbour the goods stood in a neat pile under a sheet of old sailcloth, and while Timothy went visiting a customer, Stephen Nye surreptitiously loaded boxes of tea and a keg of brandy on to the cart. He had nearly completed the task when he saw the Sergeant eyeing him from the other side of the harbour. Off went the Sergeant, as if he was shot from a gun, up the High Street, looking down every turning and alley for his superior. He must have found him, for when Timothy arrived back at the door of the shop, there stood the Captain jovially chatting to Mrs Wiseman. Then, seeing the shop had a customer, and Mr Wiseman was leaving the cart in his wife's hands to serve at the counter, the Captain actually offered to help unload the cart.

"Why, that is kind of you, sir. I don't know what we did without you and that nice sergeant of yours in the village. I'm afraid these cheeses are rather heavy, and the sugar sacks too. Maybe your sergeant ought to help you."

"No trouble at all, ma'm," proffered the all too friendly officer.

Timothy was getting a little hot and bothered at the presence of the Captain, and seeing him actually helping to unload the cart caused him not a little concern, but Mrs Wiseman was not the wife of a Wiseman in name only; she had her plan all worked out. The Captain returned, puffing a little but assuring her that this was "Nothing at all, ma'm, nothing at all" as he struggled to get a large, round cheese to the edge of the cart's tailgate. Mrs Wiseman hoisted herself up on to the cart, and she helped by turning the cheese over so that it would roll nicely and jostling it to the place where it could be taken in the arms of both men. Then, as they turned to get into position, she gave the cheese a mighty push with her foot. It left the back of the cart as if catapulted, and, as the Captain and his man held out their arms, it fairly sailed between them. Mrs Wiseman screamed at them for letting it drop, and both men went after the recalcitrant cheese, which rolled ever faster down the High Street past amazed shoppers on that fair morning in Lower Penzle.

Some laughed when they saw who were the competitors in the race; others called out encouragement as both men stumbled against each other, lunging at the cheese as it careered first left, then right, and finally rushed in through the undertaker's workshop door and came to rest under his bench.

Jonathan Peirpoint wasn't fortunate enough to see who won the race, but he was a little mystified when he entered his workshop and saw the rear ends of the Captain and the Sergeant protruding from his bench, struggling with something, either dead or alive, underneath it.

All this time Timothy and his shop boy were blissfully unloading the cart and delivering the keg to its owner down at the White Horses.

That evening, as the Captain and the Sergeant reviewed the day, dinner was served. Sergeant Sigrose dutifully left Willoughby Williams to himself and made his way to the back room where his meal was served. It was just then that something stirred in the Captain's heart as he heard the innkeeper offer him some brandy.

"I can recommend it, sir – fresh from Burgundy, I believe, and as pretty a colour as ever I've seen."

"Bah!" said the Captain under his breath. "I wouldn't mind betting that this came in from the good ship *Sea Winkle* this very week – and no tax on its merry contents, I'll be bound!"

But the Captain had great difficulty in seeing it to be his duty to spoil a good meal with such thoughts. He pushed them from his mind and, as there was no one with whom he could bet, he savoured his glass and dropped into a well-earned slumber. He had served his King and country all day. Now this last hour by a comfortable fire was his to enjoy.

"The man was right, and not only about the colour: it was indeed a good drop of brandy. And, the cheese wasn't bad, either. Oh, drat that cheesezzzz!"

CHAPTER TEN

Tea at the Windmill

Henry Gritton was miller up at Windy Ridge on the high road leading out of Lower Penzle. The mill was one of the highest points, and Henry was always busy grinding corn from farms for miles around. Everyone knew Henry, and Henry knew everyone. He had heard gossip about the smugglers, though there was little told abroad, for the well-kept secret hid the identity of the men concerned. The failure of the Captain to disrupt their activities was the main talking point, and the rector's call today was yet another occasion for laughter to ring out like the church bells had done some weeks before.

"Rector," said Henry in his usual slow, thoughtful voice, "tell me what you think about these stories of smuggling? They sound far-fetched – the sort of tales m'father used to tell. Would you support such a venture if it could bring down those taxes you've often complained about?"

The rector looked up from studying the end of his walking stick, and he looked out across the windswept bay. Without attempting to answer the miller, he himself asked a question.

"Henry, how much tax is there on a bag of flour?"

"A penny ha'penny, as it stands just now, rector."

"Henry, if that were doubled, and you knew that half of it was not going to the King, but into a greedy tax collector's pocket, what would you do?"

"Oh, I don't have to think about that, rector: I would not grind so much corn – at least, I would not do it in public, like! But, if you're asking if tax on flour is like them wretched import taxes, I can answer you straight. I know what the tax should be, from me uncle who mills over at West Yatton up in Devon, and I made that known to Richard Crendon when he came to see me two years ago. He ain't never troubled me since."

"Quite!" said the rector, slowly rising and walking to the window. "I think you've answered your own question, Henry."

"Rector, let me put my question another way, then. I'm interested in breaking Crendon's hold on this part of the country. Somewhere the King's name has got to be retrieved from its disrepute and Crendon made to behave honestly. I would do anything to help bring about this man's downfall – and that includes helping those smugglers, if they really exist."

The rector nodded without answering. He walked back to Henry's bent figure, leaning over the large wooden cogwheels, tightening a bolt down in the very centre of the great mill's internal organs. Putting a hand on those powerful shoulders, he spoke as softly as if the Captain were in the next room.

"Henry, what exactly do you know about our friends the smugglers? Do I sense that you know a little more than you are telling me?"

"Rector, if I looked up now, I think I would be looking into the face of one of them!"

The rector was torn between his loyalty to his parish men and his love for this great hulk of a Methodist, with whom he had so often talked on sacred things. So, he played along with Henry's thought.

"And what would you say or do if I were to tell you that I was the leader of that mysterious band of ghostly sailors? I suppose you would think me a traitor to my principles and an unworthy preacher of honesty and godliness. You just couldn't see your own John Wesley riding out in the night to save the tax on a keg of spirits, could you?"

"That's for sure," chuckled the miller as he heaved his weight from his task. "Come down and we'll talk over tea."

They had no sooner entered the kitchen than there was a knock at the door.

Looking out of the window, Mrs Gritton spied the panting, red-faced form of the Captain.

'Why, what would our friend, the Captain, want with you, Henry? He's never been up here before.'

Henry didn't know, but he told his wife to let the good man in, and, while she went to the door of the mill to admit the visitor, the miller asked the rector if he wished to stay for the conversation.

"I think, if I might be so bold as to suggest it, I would like to stay for the conversation; but I don't want to be seen here!"

"Right, rector, step into my office right there."

This done, the Captain came into the room. Mrs Gritton thought for a moment that the rector must have gone to wash his hands for tea, but Henry signalled that she was not to mention his presence. She busied herself with preparing for her new guest as if they had been alone till he came.

"I've never been to your worthy establishment before, miller," said the little man, puffing as if getting up steam. "I'm interested in this fine vantage point you have, for a lookout over the sea."

"Well, yes, sir, we have one of the finest views from up here, and this old mill fair rocks like a ship itself when a storm blows."

"I would like to come up and spend a night here, if that's all right with your good self," said the Captain in the clipped tones of a command.

"Well, I've no objections, as long as you don't start milling some of my corn in the middle of the night. I heard your escapade in the church belfry was a little noisy, sir."

The Captain coughed and spluttered as Mrs Gritton set down the tea, and she almost dropped the tray as she realised what Henry had said.

"I will behave myself as an officer of His Majesty's army should, I assure you, my good man, and I'll ask you to remember that what I do in the course of duty is not yours nor anybody else's business!"

It was obviously a painful subject that Henry had raised, and the conversation dropped on to more congenial matters for the Captain. Soon tea was served, together with freshly baked scones and cream.

The Captain tucked his handkerchief into his collar and tucked in to his scones as if he had just completed a ten-mile route march at the front of his men. Captain Williams coughed as a crumb got stuck in his throat, and Mrs Gritton served him a third cup of tea.

"My man," said the Captain, addressing the miller as if he were about to complain about last week's grinding, "I believe you are a Methodist?"

"Yes, sir, I am. You ask the question as if it were a crime in these parts."

"On the contrary, my good fellow, on the contrary! I am pleased to find a man who will give me an honest opinion on the Anglican rector of this parish."

Henry's hair tingled at the back of his neck, and Mrs Gritton blushed a little. She complained that her tea was a little too hot, and she said she would have to cool it with a little fresh milk from the kitchen.

"I want your honest opinion, my man, as a Methodist, and as a subject of the Crown."

Henry collected his scattered thoughts and addressed the Captain in no uncertain way.

"Sir, I am unashamedly a Methodist. My father was founder of the society in these parts, and I gladly follow in his godly footsteps. I think it no crime and no disloyalty to the person of His Majesty the King to be a Nonconformist."

The Captain had not bargained for this defence of the Dissenters, and he was quite nonplussed by the miller's remarks.

At that moment, another person joined them at the tea table, and the Captain knew not whether to drop his cup or swallow whole his mouthful of scone. As it was, he caught his breath, coughed, and delivered scone to most parts of the table in the process.

"Rector, I think you have met the King's officer. As you heard, he was enquiring after you in a most personal manner. No doubt you can answer his question yourself as you walk down the hill together. I have to get ready for the prayer meeting in half an hour from now at the chapel.

CHAPTER ELEVEN

A Life on the Ocean Wave

The *Sea Winkle* was as seaworthy as ships come, and the fact that she was an elderly lady of the sea did not deter Captain Storeton from taking her out in all weathers. Sometimes she was a little sluggish in a strong swell, and this made her later than usual today. She should have rounded the headland into the bay at a little after eleven o'clock to be ready for the smugglers to pick up their goods an hour later if the wind was keen. However, they had already been in position for an hour when they heard a distant clock ring out one o'clock. It was then that the weather really broke on them. There was a flash of lightning and a slow peal of thunder and, as the wind freshened to seaward, the rain began.

It was the keen eye of Peter Simple that saw the other boat – not the *Sea Winkle* out beyond them, but another small boat – tossing not 200 yards from them.

"Aha! Mr Simple, we have company, then," called the rector through the hissing of the rain on their waterproofs. "Methinks we may not be making a collection tonight. Let's pull out to sea a little and watch what happens."

In the second boat things were not so orderly, nor the eyesight so good. Captain Williams and his sergeant had decided that this night they were not going to be fooled nor made to wait till the morning to see evidence of smuggling which they could never prove. Here they would be on the scene to catch the smugglers in the very act of transferring their booty from the ship. Neither the Captain nor the Sergeant were seamen, but they had been practising for days and they had already developed some skill in handling their light craft even when wind, rain, and a heavy swell made it not too easy for a seasoned seaman to hold course. Captain Williams was steersman and the poor sergeant, already sick in the stomach, was pulling on the oars as well as he could. They had set out earlier than the smugglers, but they had taken much longer to row single-handed to this spot. The question in the Captain's mind was where exactly was the pickup made? It could be a mile or two in any direction. One thing he had observed was that on the night the *Sea Winkle* came in a light was flashed. This he had seen from both the church tower and the windmill. Tonight he was ready. If there were no smugglers out here (and he had not seen another boat besides his), he would at least answer the *Sea Winkle*'s lantern and catch the captain of that worthy ship in the act as he handed him the contraband. The plan seemed foolproof, except that the *Sea Winkle* was late, very late, and Sergeant Sigrose was sick, very sick.

"Keep those oars steady, sir," bellowed Captain Williams. "You'll have us turn over if we get broadside on one of these swells."

The other man had little mind for obedience to his superior at this moment, and even the shadowy sight of a black hull and a tall sail did not rouse him from his growing misery.

"Can't we go home, sir? Oh, sir, won't you take over for a while? You can threaten to court-martial me, shoot me, and bury me at sea, but I can't row another yard!"

With those words he crumpled forward and gave evidence that his sickness was not of the sham variety.

Captain Williams had no intention of giving up, even though by now even he was willing to admit this was not where he wanted to be. Just then, a light flashed out from the heaving ship, coming now at some speed with a fair wind in her sails.

"Ah, just what I've been waiting for – one, two, three, four, five, six flashes. Right, my friend, Mr Storeton, two can play at that game."

The Captain lifted, with not too steady a hand, the lantern he had carefully set in the stern of his craft. He answered flash for flash – all six of them – and waited. Captain Storeton counted those answering flashes and waited for the seventh which should have come; but there were only six. Willoughby Williams knew nothing of this code, and he almost sat on the Sergeant's heaving form as he took the oars and rowed towards the oncoming *Sea Winkle*. The ship and boat were side by side in a moment, and a rope was thrown down to the tossing small boat.

"Ahoy there!" said Poulton, the first mate. "Is there something you fishermen are wanting?"

Captain Williams had no idea what the usual procedure was, but he called for Captain Storeton and the goods!

Just at this time, at the seaward side of the *Sea Winkle*, another light flashed evenly seven times, twice repeated. Captain Storeton, though, hurried to the landward side of the ship and asked who was there. Captain Williams, now unable to disguise himself, shouted in his most military voice that he was an officer of the King. He said that he had observed a signal, had answered it, and deduced that there was something fishy going on.

"You are dead right: there is something fishy going on, Captain Williams. We have something for you, if you are the one sent to pick it up."

And, with that, he lowered over the side and into the waiting arms of the Captain a basket of fresh mackerel. This done, he bade the Captain good night and called for the line to be pulled aboard as the *Sea Winkle* went on her way. As she went, the rector's boat on the seaward side pulled hard away into the darkness. The poor sergeant, already sick and helpless in the bottom of the other boat, caught the whole basket of fish as the Captain lost his grip and reached for the oars.

It was with difficulty, but mad determination, that Captain Williams rowed himself and his sick companion towards the harbour lights of Lower Penzle. He said nothing the whole way; Sergeant Sigrose was beyond conversation as he slithered among the still-wriggling fish in the sloshing bilge of the boat.

The second boat made its way steadily at a distance behind the first, and only as the two boats neared the harbour entrance did the rector call out a greeting:

"Ahoy there, Captain Williams, sir! I had no idea you were a nocturnal fisherman. Did you catch anything tonight? I would be guilty of the sin of jealousy if you did, for we had a mighty poor night ourselves."

"Yes, rector, I did catch more fish than I'd hoped for. And 'twill last me many a long night too."

"Well done, sir!" chorused the crew of the second boat as they rowed swiftly to the far side of the harbour and carefully unloaded their catch for the night – three cases of tea, a half-keg of brandy, and two heavy sacks of rice.

"Not such a disappointing catch, gentlemen!" called the rector in a loud voice as they all made their way up the harbour and separated to go to their homes.

Captain Willoughby Williams had his problems. One was a big hulk of humanity that did not move from the floor of the boat, even at the threat of being shot at dawn; and the other was a basket of fresh mackerel that covered him and his companion with smell enough to have every cat in Lower Penzle follow them home to bed.

The one question Captain Williams never answered about that night was the one Joshua Pendle asked the following morning – namely, what bait had he used to catch such a fine basket of fish?

CHAPTER TWELVE

The Miller's Sense of Humour

As we have said, Henry Gritton, miller to the countryside around Lower Penzle, was a Methodist. He was, in fact, as zealous a Methodist as you might find in the West Country, often setting out early on a Sabbath morning to preach at a far-off cottage meeting of John Wesley's followers. As such, he had little to do with the parish affairs of Lower Penzle. The new rector, however, often stopped by for a chat on spiritual matters, feeling a keen kinship for the vital religion of this muscular man of the mill. Already the two had met on eye-to-eye terms regarding the smugglers' work, and a deep understanding had developed between them. An altogether new relationship was opening up between the Methodist and Anglican communions, so to speak.

Captain Williams had not missed a move of the rector's for weeks. Every meeting of the parish council had been monitored, and already a couple of shipments of contraband had been missed because of his watchful eye. Such a cat-and-mouse game could not be allowed to continue. Another move must be made, and that soon, if Sir Richard Crendon was not to win the day. The mill and the miller seemed to provide a possible solution. Calling in on his Methodist friend, the rector suggested that the parish council might be allowed to meet at the mill for its next extraordinary meeting on Wednesday night. There was a full moon, and Captain Williams was certain to be out on patrol, if not on duty in the rectory garden itself.

So it was that, on Wednesday at half past six, two parish councillors were seen slowly walking up the high road to Windy Ridge. It was dark before the next two set off, and by the time Old Joseph was collected by Timothy Wiseman in his cart, all the rest were enjoying fresh bread and newly pressed farmhouse cheese in the miller's parlour. The rector was last to arrive, and he was somewhat perturbed by the fact that Sergeant Sigrose had seen him on the way. The Sergeant seemed to be too obviously on the lookout for the rector's ease. Had the Captain discovered the new venue? There was no possibility of a traitor among this group. It was, in fact, a coincidence that had led the Sergeant to overhear two of the councillors making final arrangements, and, unbeknown to anyone, the Captain was already on his way up the hill to snoop around the mill.

The tightly closed shutters creaked in the wind which never seemed to leave the hilltop. The sails of the great mill were still, however, for Henry had the brakes on the great machinery. From an upper window of the mill, Mrs Gritton spied the glint of a bright buckle, or button, as the scudding clouds let a fleeting shaft of moonlight catch the dress of a man standing a little way off from the lower end of one of the sails. She quietly opened the upper casement and listened. There was no mistaking the heavy breathing of the Captain, obviously hot from his fast walk up the high road. Leaving the window on the latch, she went downstairs to the large kitchen. There, around the scrubbed tabletop, sat the parish council with the Methodist miller in attendance. His broad smile showed how pleased he was with the fact that his sympathies had bridged any gap that might have separated him in churchmanship. He was one with these men; he had no doubt of the justice of their action.

They had not started on the real business of the evening when Molly Gritton coughed and waited to be heard. Quietly she whispered, as if she feared to be overheard by the Captain out in the breezy night.

"We have a visitor, gentlemen; our esteemed representative of the law stands in the shadow of the sails."

"Does he, now?" responded the miller, getting up from his seat in the chimney corner, from where he had been an active participant in the council meeting. He followed Molly up the stairs, and from the casement he observed the panting King's man, his coat now open and blowing in the wind like a great cloak rather than part of a tailored military uniform. As they watched, Captain Williams first mopped his brow, then removed his coat. This he placed upon the nearest resting place he could find – the lower end of the great windmill sail, which at this point was just within reach of his short arms. Leaving it thus suspended, he moved forward on his task of investigation. He made for the kitchen window where, shuttered though it was, he would surely be able to make out the voices within.

"Haste 'ee down and inform the rector. Take them all through into the mill. I have a little matter to attend to in the machine room."

The Captain, meanwhile, was tiptoeing, like some ballet dancer, through the moonlight towards the kitchen window. Almost imperceptibly, behind him the great sail of the mill moved in the wind. The miller having taken the pressure off the brake, the great sails responded to the pull of the breeze and turned just half a circle. But that half-circle was enough to carry the coat of the Captain high into the night sky and far out of reach. Still unaware of his coat's elevation, the Captain peeped in through the slatted shutters. The light made him squint, but, as his eyes became accustomed to the bright lamps on wall and table, he was not a little surprised to see none but the miller's wife quietly darning a very large hole in her husband's thickest woollen socks. He circled the whole building, peering here and there into the dark rooms he passed, but all the time missing the eyes that were peering out at him from the mill's first floor.

He turned, hissing under his breath, and walked carefully across the gravel to where he had left his coat. The sail was there, at the very same point where he had hung his coat, but no coat was to be seen. Not, that is, until the moon came out again, and there, flying like a pennant in the night breeze, was his coat, full ninety feet above the ground.

He gasped! "How in the world did it get up there?" he asked himself out loud, and, as if in answer to his question, a voice said, "I'm over here, sir!"

It was Sergeant Sigrose.

Quick as a night owl swooping on its prey, the Captain pounced on his assistant. In a hoarse stage whisper, he pointed to the flying coat and said, "Get that thing down here, Sergeant. Do you hear me? Get it down here, or we'll be the laughing stock of the miller and anyone he cares to tell his tale to."

"But I've no head for heights, sir," remonstrated the terrified sergeant, contemplating a cracked skull and fractured arms and legs.

"I'll help you on to the lower sail, and you can climb up to the centre and then up to my coat."

Remonstrate he did, but his training took command, and, before he knew what he was really doing, Sergeant Egbert Sigrose obeyed. He took his first feeble steps up the ladder-like sails of the great mill.

This scene was being watched by fourteen good men, and they had now been joined by a worthy woman. Not one of those onlookers had a hand to spare. With one hand they stifled their laughter, and with the other they held their sides. None had seen the like in years – no, not at the fair nor at the travelling jesters' best market-day show. This was a story each would have the utmost difficulty in keeping secret. But the end of the miller's humour was not yet. As poor Sigrose inched his way up the sail, the Captain all the while whispering that he was "right behind him", the miller slipped back to his machinery and again released the brake a fraction. The great sail began to move, an inch at a time, and even Sigrose was unaware of its movement. Little by little, however, he became aware that he was not now climbing up so much as going sideways. The ground had somehow moved.

The Captain was no longer below him, and his descent to the ground seemed completely cut off. What was happening? He did not know, but obedience to the command from below was still the instinct which drove each shuddering movement of his weak limbs. Slowly he climbed, and slowly the miller let the great sails turn their full circle, so, by the time Sigrose was halfway along the second sail, he was actually climbing down. The coat was now within reach of the Captain himself, and poor Sigrose was quite disoriented.

"Hurry up and get down before you go all the way round again," hoarsely whispered Captain Williams, donning his coat and hurrying off down the hill.

This had been yet another abortive attempt to catch the smugglers. Would he ever get even with them, he wondered.

Inside the mill, the merriment had died down; and the meeting concluded with plans for the next attempt to collect contraband from the *Sea Winkle*.

CHAPTER THIRTEEN

The Magic of the Midnight Hour

Captain Willoughby Williams did not find his duties at Lower Penzle as arduous as one might think. True, he seemed no nearer to catching the smugglers, though he was more sure than ever that he had identified their leader and an accomplice or two. His occasional visits to Crendon Hall were not the happiest occasions, for he had very little to show for his time and efforts. Sir Richard's one consolation was that very little of the *Sea Winkle*'s cargo had got through; and the Captain and the Sergeant were surely as good a deterrent as could be placed in Lower Penzle.

'Perhaps prevention is better than cure,' he told himself.

On the lighter side of Captain Williams' duties were the social calls he made in the course of his investigation in the hope that an unguarded word here or there would lead him to the smugglers. These calls the astute officer made at appropriate and convenient hours. It seemed he knew just when was the day on which each middle-aged widow or busy housewife did her baking. A day might, if he timed his visits well, yield him a couple of fresh scones here and a toasted teacake there, not to mention a fair slice of apple pie at Widow Adams' back kitchen table. She enjoyed his flattery, and he had a fair enough supply when it produced such delicious results.

He was nicely seated on just such an occasion, and the smell from the baking in the oven was enough to make a proposal of marriage the order of the day. However, if a few kind words would produce the same large portion of whatever was cooking, he would make do with that.

Widow Adams busied herself tidying up her kitchen. Flour was everywhere, and the Captain's coat sleeves were already looking a trifle like a newly bathed and powdered baby. He coughed a little, nervous cough, and chuckled in childlike anticipation of the opening of the oven door. The moment arrived, but disappeared again as the expert cook decided the contents were not quite ready for serving.

"Madam, I do declare that you keep a man in suspense till he can hardly contain his appetite."

"Well, I know you must be a busy man, Captain Williams. It is so good of you to call on an old widow woman, and I do so appreciate your good sergeant's chopping the wood for my stove. I've baked a little extra for him too this morning, so I hope I'm not asking too much of his superior officer to carry it to him."

"Well, madam, I do not usually carry for my man, but, seeing as you ask me, I will not deny him such a small treat as you may reward him with. Of course, the King's men need no such reward for duties performed in His Majesty's name."

"Oh, Lor! I do hope my little kindnesses are not against the law, sir. I wouldn't like to disturb your conscience, like!"

"Why, bless you, madam, such a thought was furthest from my mind. But I was just saying that you do not need to burden yourself with Sergeant Sigrose. He is well looked after at the inn. I sometimes have to remind him that he lives in the lap of luxury compared to the men in barracks."

"Quite, quite, Captain," concluded Widow Adams as she put her mind to carefully lifting the steaming pies on to the kitchen table. The Captain's eyes stood out like organ stops and his mouth dribbled saliva, causing him to dab it at both sides to keep himself from spluttering his premature gratitude for such a large slice.

Not a word was spoken as, with knife and fork, he made his attack in true military style upon the outer perimeter of the piecrust. Strong breathing, spluttering and munching finally gave way to a great "Ah!" of contentment and congratulation.

"It was, madam, the finest you have ever allowed me to taste! You are an excellent cook, madam. I wonder that your widowhood has continued so long. The very smell should bring a host of suitors to your back door, if I don't embarrass you by saying so, madam."

"Bless you, sir! You do not embarrass me, but I have had three husbands, you know, and none lived to enjoy much of m'cooking. Poor Adams only lived a year and died of gout. He wasn't young, of course, but I did hope he might have lasted a bit longer after all the promises he made. Then Edwards wasn't much better. He left me after just three years, and most of that time he was away at sea and couldn't enjoy my cooking; he always said he enjoyed his ship food as much as anything I cooked."

"That, madam, was most ungrateful and unkind. I dare to say that he did not deserve the good offices of such a wife. That piecrust was the essence of delight. I suppose there might not be a slither or two more to spare?"

"Why, let me wrap the rest of it up for you. I'm sure you could eat it as well cold to keep you fed these cold nights when you're out after them smugglers."

"Madam, I must not inform you of my nocturnal duties, but I will say that tonight promises to be a cold one, and even in a graveyard a piece of that pie would taste a treat in the early hours of the morning."

"Bless my soul! You don't mean you have to keep watch over the dead?"

"Well, not exactly, madam, but, between you and me, we do have to keep a lookout in the most unlikely places."

Widow Adams made her way up the High Street, and, after

collecting half an ounce of wool at the clothing store, she stood chatting to Mrs Wiseman as the good grocer's wife weighed out a pound and a half of fresh dairy butter. By the time she had finished patting and chopping, dipped the wooden pats into water, and wrapped the bright-yellow produce, the grocer's wife had heard all that the Captain had said and more. Timothy Wiseman was all for making the Captain's visit to the graveyard at the church a worthwhile time. There was a reason more valid than the Captain could know for him to search for evidence of smuggling. The last boat trip had left the smugglers with more than they could dispose of right away, and it had not been thought a desecration by the rector that certain casks should be stored under a stone vault till they could be secretly transported to Crendon Bywater.

At something after twelve that night, two men stood in the lee of the church tower, buttoned up to their noses. They looked like statues, if rather odd and mismatched ones. From their collars issued the steam of breath condensing in the chill night air. From his pocket, the Captain drew a large, red handkerchief. Stepping forward to the nearest tombstone vault, he carefully placed the little bundle before him and proceeded to untie the knot. There before the men lay two large slices of apple pie. Cold and without the added sprinkle of sugar, they still looked good in the half-light that filtered through from the clouded moon. Before either man had stretched his hand to touch whichever piece might be the larger, an owl hooted above their heads. The Sergeant jumped and grasped his superior officer's coat sleeve. The Captain clutched his collar and pulled it even further up the back of his neck.

Now both men looked back at their pieces of pie at the same moment, and both looked at each other accusingly. There was but one piece before their incredulous eyes. But it was obvious to both that if they had taken it, they had not eaten it, because as they spoke their mouths were all too empty.

"Where in the world did that go to?" asked Captain Williams almost under his breath. "If there are rats in this here churchyard, then they are mighty swift ones."

With that, he took up the remaining piece and selflessly divided it in two. He placed it down, and, as he did so, there was a thud behind them that made them nearly fall over the tomb on which their repast was spread. They turned to inspect the grass behind them and found nothing more than a large stone. Where it had come from they had no idea, but they were beginning to get jumpy.

"Let's eat up and go round to the other side of the church," said the Captain, unashamedly nervous in his haste.

But when they looked back at their pie, there was but one piece left. Picking it up, indignant and mystified, the Captain bit into it, as far as the size of his mouth would allow him, and handed the other piece to his companion. Without a word Sergeant Sigrose took what he was offered as though taking Communion from a priest. His mouth, being of the larger variety, was able to accommodate his piece with ease, in spite of the fact that it was more crust than apple. The Captain, without looking, felt for his handkerchief, but it was nowhere to be found.

"Sigrose, did you take my kerchief?"

"Me, sir?"

"Well, if you didn't, who did? Rats don't use handkerchiefs to my knowledge, and there's not enough wind to rustle the trees. I've had enough of this place. We'll go and sit in the church porch. Come on – this way!"

The two men stumbled their way round the chancel end of the church, and, after tripping over numerous bushes and broken tombs, they almost fell on to the little wooden seat in the entrance porch. The Captain unbuttoned his collar and eased himself back on the seat, a hand on each side of him. His left hand touched cloth on the seat beside him. He picked it up and shuddered. It was his handkerchief.

"How – how in the world did that get from the other side of the church to here?"

"I don't know, and I don't care, sir. I've had enough for one night. We ain't seen or heard a thing, but if we stay here these ghosts are going to strip us naked and leave us for dead. I'm for going home right now."

"Ghosts? Ghosts? You surely do not sit there and tell me that a grown man and a soldier believes that what we have been the victims of is a ghost?"

Before the Sergeant had a chance to explain his belief in the metaphysical, the church door opened wide and then slammed with such force that it was like a cannon going off in the ears of the two poor men. Cannon-like they were projected into the night and both half ran, half stumbled into the lane before they knew why they had moved. They did not speak as they slowed to a walk, but Sergeant Sigrose felt somehow he had a convert to his way of explaining the happenings of the night, while down from the church tower and up from under a tombstone seat shuffled two undignified members of the parish council on their way home to a well-earned sleep.

CHAPTER FOURTEEN

Burial at Sea

The sloping bilge boards of the long boat were never designed with the long, flowing skirts of a lady in mind, and it was obvious that Mrs Grundle was not the usual seagoing type. Her husband, on the other hand, had been at sea more than on the land, and she had brought all four of her boys up almost single-handedly while her husband had been roving the wide seas of the world. Ben Grundle had always returned with some tale of great adventure, and Mrs Grundle had listened, but she had never been tempted by his alluring stories of sunlit isles and waving palms. Her delight was the fireside of their harbour cottage (No. 3), which had been her home since marriage. In fact, they had spent their two-day honeymoon there before Ben had had to join his ship at Plymouth for another long voyage away. Their first baby was three months old when he returned, and life had followed this pattern for them both. His very last trip away had ended some ten years before. From that trip he brought home his other love. If he was the typical seaman in many respects, one thing is certain: he did not have wife nor girlfriend anywhere else in the world but Lower Penzle. Betsy was his first and only girl. It had been a whirlwind courtship, and a marriage that everyone advised against, but it had lasted. Now, in their retirement, they were still the sweethearts of the village, sitting in the summer evenings on the harbourside, unashamedly holding hands as the sun went down on their silver heads.

It was Salty, the scraggy little dog he had brought home from that last trip, that had caused Betsy to set sail this afternoon. Ben had been sick with bronchitis these many months, and it seemed he would never pull through. Some nights he would wheeze like a whistle. Curled up on the foot of his bed, right through his illness, Salty had hardly left her post as guardian of her master. The whole village mourned when little Salty stretched out one evening, yawned, shuddered and lay still – very, very still. It was a tragedy. Old Ben moved his feet in the bed, but Salty never raised her little ruffled head to look up at her master. She had departed this life for the long voyage that has no return. Old Ben cried like a baby, and so did his eldest son as they stroked the little body, still warm but not breathing. Salty was dead.

"I've just one great regret," cried Ben as he told the rector of his loss.

"And what might that be, Ben?"

"I promised Salty that when the end came, if she went before me, I would give her a proper burial at sea where she was born. The poor old thing won't know no difference now, but I would like to keep my promise."

The rector sat silent for a few moments and looked thoughtfully at old Ben.

"Ben, my old friend, you shall keep your promise and do us of the parish council a right good favour at the same time.

"Rector, am I reading your thoughts aright? Are you thinking of taking my Salty out one night to meet the *Sea Winkle*?"

"Meeting the *Sea Winkle* is right, Ben, but not at night. The *Sea Winkle* has been later these winter days, and daylight is not very helpful to our little welcome party, as you well know. No, we shall meet the *Sea Winkle* in broad daylight and Salty will keep guard to see no one intrudes upon a burial at sea!"

That is how Mrs Betsy Grundle came to be sitting right there in the centre of two burly rowers and looking into the face of the rector at the stern of the long boat. As it cut through the choppy waters at the harbour entrance, the Captain, spyglass held behind him, watched them leave for the open sea. The precious cargo lay there between Betsy and the man ahead of her – a small coffin with a simple inscription on its cover: 'Salty, faithful to the end, born at sea, to the sea committed' and the dates of her birth and death. Jonathan Peirpoint had made the little casket in honour of his friend, Ben, glad that it was not for the man himself, for all respected and held him in high esteem. Many villagers were down at the harbour, and it was not just the wind that caused an eye to water that keen winter afternoon as Betsy made her pilgrimage.

There was another plan being fulfilled at this time also. For as the Captain waited and watched the tossing little boat he spied the *Sea Winkle* as it came round the point.

"By all the cunning in the kingdom," he thought out loud, "I do believe the rector is mixing business with pleasure. If that be the case, I shall be here to assist Betsy Grundle up the harbour steps myself, indeed I will."

The two boats drew near to each other and lines were exchanged. Betsy was plainly seen by the Captain to climb aboard the *Sea Winkle*, and the rector also.

"So that's the daring plan – is it? – to get the cargo ashore at Crendon Bywater under the very noses of the law. We'll catch 'em red-handed, we will!"

Captain Williams waited not a minute longer but hurried up the harbour to the inn. There he hired a horse, and away he rode towards Crendon Bywater at a fair pace. Had he waited long enough, he would have seen a lantern signal flash an all-clear across the waves. And, as Mrs Betsy Grundle settled for the voyage to Crendon Bywater, with the little ceremony on the way, Mr Poulton handed down four boxes of tea and a roll or two of cloth.

The two boats parted, and the *Sea Winkle* made her way beyond the point. Even as she sailed, tossing and pitching into the open sea, the rector called above the noise of the wind in the rigging a brief but thoughtful committal, and the small coffin was slid out over the side. With a gentle splash, it disappeared beneath the waves for ever.

No one was more surprised to see Captain Williams standing on the harbour wall at Crendon Bywater than Mrs Betsy Grundle, and no one was more watchful of her companion than he. But look as he would, and assisted as he was by watchful assistants, there was just nothing irregular about the unloading of the *Sea Winkle* that evening.

After a hot drink, the rector escorted his charge to a pony trap, and, their mission complete, three quiet people rode home to Lower Penzle to inform Ben Grundle that his last promise to his dog had been kept to the letter. She had been buried at sea.

CHAPTER FIFTEEN

Sacrilege

Ben Pearson's old cart trundled into the backyard of Jonathan Peirpoint's funeral establishment, and Ben tied his horse securely before entering the workshop. The smell of new wood was everywhere, and a couple of the finest coffins stood up on end like wardrobes waiting for new clothes.

Ben's voice rang through the corners of the lofty building and quickly brought Jonathan scurrying from his house door.

"Ben, that voice will wake my clients from the dead," chuckled Jonathan as he took Ben by the arm and led him into the house from the workshop.

Ben said nothing in reply – if, indeed, he had heard the remark! He was not fond of the Peirpoints' trade, and he avoided anything more than a stop outside when he delivered wood from Crendon Bywater, but today he had been asked to take something on the return journey. When he learned what it was, he got up to go without giving a reply. Jonathan grabbed his arm.

"Now, now, Ben! You're not going to refuse a little favour, are you? All I ask is that you take the body, and I will meet you at Crendon Bywater Church."

"What I want to know is, why can't it be taken in the hearse like any other decent burial?"

"Well, Ben, I have another funeral at Crendon tomorrow,

and I have to take the coffin there this afternoon. I can't deliver a coffin on your cart, but I can meet you at a respectable distance from the church and take the body from you for the funeral there today. You know old Dick Savage hasn't a relative here or there, but there is a grave for him if I can get his coffin there before three this afternoon. Come on, now! Surely you would want someone to do the same for you one day!"

"I ain't even thinking of that day," bellowed old Ben, "and when it do come, you can do what you likes. I'll not be paying no bills for whatever you does! You'll get no profit from my funeral."

"It's a deal, then, Ben: five shillings when we meet at Crendon Bywater Church – on the west side, mind you. I don't want no public viewing of this little exchange. I have my good name to protect in such delicate matters as transporting in a reverent manner – even if it is only old Dick Savage."

Ben gave unwilling assistance to Jonathan and his son as they lifted the not too heavy coffin on to Ben's old cart and covered it with a heavy sack or two. Then Ben trundled his heaven-bound cargo to the White Horses, where he planned to take his dinner in style on the strength of his well-earned five shillings – a princely sum for a single journey. His presence in the White Horses was so rare a sight that the Captain left his usual table by the fire and sat on the good-ear side of the deaf old carter – if one ear really was any better than the other!

"I see you're loaded for a journey, my good fellow," said Captain Williams with as casual an air as you can put into a shout down a deaf man's ear.

Ben stuffed another mouthful of pickled onions beside his bread and cheese before answering. The mumbled reply was hardly intelligible and showered Willoughby Williams with both sight and smell of the inn's best food. The Captain was ever watchful of everything that went on the high road from Lower Penzle to Crendon Bywater, but somehow the smugglers managed to get their contraband past every trap he set. A passing thought caused Willoughby Williams to leave the table before Ben had time to empty his mouth.

"Give Ben a pint of ale with my compliments, will you?" the Captain whispered to the barmaid as he left.

He buttoned up his topcoat against the wind and almost tiptoed out to where Ben's old mare stood champing at her bit and munching the last of her nosebag dinner. He lifted the sack, and what he saw took him by surprise. The rough coffin, a meagre last home for Dick Savage, supplied by the parish, was all the cart contained.

'But why should the undertaker send a coffin by cart and not take it himself?'

Captain Willoughby Williams racked his brains and arrived at a daring conclusion. He shared his thoughts with Sergeant Sigrose, and together they set out along the high road out of Lower Penzle. Passing the undertaker's, the Captain saw Jonathan Peirpoint loading his hearse, and that confirmed all that he was thinking.

"We're right, my man – we're as right as we've ever been, and we shall catch our friends red-handed. What say you, Sergeant Sigrose?"

"I say that we ought to be catching our enemies red-handed, sir, if you ask me!"

"Oh, you know what I mean. You sometimes are as dumb as your horse!"

The two men rode up the hill into the wind and made their way to a crossroads where they could shelter in a small copse and await their moment.

It was a quarter to two when Ben's old mare high-stepped her way up to the crossroads. Like two highwaymen, the Captain and the Sergeant rode out to head off this 'heaven-bound mail'. Ben looked up from his position, staring at the rump of his mare.

"What do you think you're a-doing of?" Ben cried as he reigned in his frightened animal.

She shied and pawed at the ground as the old carter held her still. The wind was keen and Ben was annoyed at being stopped. He had an appointment to be at Crendon Bywater Church, and no one would be pleased if he were late – least of all the vicar who was to conduct the service.

"My good man, we stop you in the name of the King and demand that you reveal the contents of your load."

Ben was furious at being stopped by this impudent little officer, whom he had disliked from the first day he drove him and his miserable assistant from Crendon Bywater to Lower Penzle. Ben had nothing to do with smuggling, and, although he knew well enough what the Captain was saying, his deafness grew suddenly complete.

"I don't hear what you're saying, and I haven't time to stop and listen, so out of my way and let me pass."

But before Ben could whip up his mare the Captain took firm hold of her bit and Sergeant Sigrose uncovered the contents of the cart. The Sergeant was not quite ready to see a coffin, though the Captain had told him of its presence.

"Open it up!" snapped the Captain.

"D-d-do I have to do this, sir? Surely you, as the senior officer of the King present, should officiate at such a moment of d-d-delicate investigation."

'Get on with the job. What that coffin contains will frighten no one but the smugglers in court."

Ben could just catch a word here and there and guessed at the rest. The Captain shouted at the top of his voice – a voice that was loud enough to raise the dead – and the Sergeant jumped back from his gruesome task.

"Will you get on with your duty, man!" shouted the Captain.

Sergeant Sigrose took a long screwdriver from his pocket, and his fingers trembled as if he were committing an unpardonable sin. Slowly he prised the lid upwards and then fell backwards at what he saw. The Captain turned his horse and swung around to the rear of the cart. There, in full view of the winter sky, lay Richard Samuel Savage, aged eighty-one, born 15 June, died 5 November. He was truly dead; only his nightshirt stirred in the cold wind.

"Oh dear, oh dear, oh dear, oh dear . . ." kept repeating Sergeant Sigrose as he sat on the ground behind the cart.

Captain Williams stood speechless. What was there to say? Before he could think of what to say to Ben, an even worse storm blew from the direction of Lower Penzle: the undertaker's hearse came smoothly towards them at the crossroads.

Jonathan Peirpoint guessed what the whole scene meant. He held his horse under control, but his temper was not so easily or willingly controlled. He let fly at the Captain with every word of indignation he could think of.

The Captain's face made him look like a candidate for Jonathan's personal and professional attention as he tried to explain his suspicions and state his authority for the actions he had taken, but Jonathan would have none of it. He threatened to complain about the Captain's sacrilegious act to his superior officer at Truro – and even London if need be. All the while Jonathan's son was screwing the coffin lid back in place, and when it was done he covered it again with the heavy sacking. Jonathan excused himself hurriedly, and, after shouting to Ben not to be late at Crendon Bywater Church, the hearse made its steady and speedy way to the address of Jonathan Peirpoint's next deceased customer – albeit via one or two other addresses, where small packages were left with the compliments of the smugglers.

The Vicar of Crendon Bywater was not at all pleased to be kept waiting for the Lower Penzle funeral, but he was shocked to learn that the coffin had been opened, the dead unrespected. He resolved to pass his complaints on to Sir Richard when next he visited the hall. *Sacrilegious* was the only word for it.

CHAPTER SIXTEEN

The Betrayal

How long could an escapade like this continue? When would the smugglers be caught? They themselves had asked this question many times since they set themselves to get around the injustice of Sir Richard Crendon. When the end came, no one quite expected it, and certainly not in the way it finally came. The battle of wits between the Captain and his sergeant and the smugglers had only been possible because of the extreme loyalty of those within the smugglers' circle. No one else in the village knew enough to set a trap or even give a hint as to how they might be cornered. But for some time a tempestuous friendship had been running between Lizzie Slocum and Donald Creedy. I say tempestuous, for Lizzie was as red-haired as they come and had a temper to match her fiery head. Donald was her sweetheart from schooldays, and while he had matured into a fine, responsible young man, Lizzie had not lost her childish habit of insisting on having her own way. Donald had many times freed himself from the hands of this young lady, but in a village as small as Lower Penzle it is not so easy to get out of the net, or off the hook, of so persistent an angler as Lizzie was proving to be.

He met her each Sunday at church, and she made it very obvious that no one else should sit alongside 'her' Donald. Donald himself had long since reconciled himself to his fate, and he had, to some extent, managed a little taming of the shrew. But just now the tempestuous nature of the relationship was showing itself a little more often than it had for some time.

Donald, as we have seen, was deeply involved in the smuggling fraternity. Lizzie seemed not to have the slightest suspicion, even though she showed her dislike for Donald's new love of fishing out in the bay at night. She had no love for the sea, though she had been born within sound and sight of it. She had still less liking for fishing; to her, it was a messy business which could be avoided by regular visits to the fishmonger's shop. Her present argument with Donald was over his breaking of an arrangement to meet her in favour of an evening fishing trip. How he could just put her off like this infuriated her, and she spoke her mind at home.

It happened that one evening Captain Williams was a guest at the Slocums' table. The meal was not very large – the Slocums were not renowned for their generosity. The Captain looked the meal over, and, seeing he did not have much in the food line to hold his interest, he enquired after Lizzie's romantic life. That was all that was needed to spark off a display that shocked her father and mother, as well as their guest. Lizzie let fly verbally at everyone she knew would be on this fishing trip, including the rector.

"Did you say the rector would be on the trip?" asked the Captain with a careless air.

"Yes. He always goes with them; and, if you ask me, he's a bad omen for them. They never catch much fish. They don't usually stay out long – but long enough to take my Donald away for the evening."

Captain Willoughby Williams pricked up his ears. A plan formed in his mind, and he made a suggestion which was out before he could guard what he was saying.

"I think we might be able to stop these little fishing trips, if you would help me, my dear."

"Oh, I could never stop Donald fishing. This last year he has gained such a love for it that he has time for nothing else. I sometimes think he's fallen in love with a mermaid out there."

"Now, now, my dear Miss Lizzie, you and I know that no mermaid could compete with your fair face, now, could she?"

Willoughby Williams found himself admitting inwardly that he was a liar to say so, but it was all in a good cause. He was gaining the lady's confidence and cooperation for his plan.

"All you need to do, my dear, is to let me know the next time Donald has a fishing trip arranged. Just let me know the time. I have a little plan that might make fishing trips a little less palatable for him. Maybe you will have your Donald at home a little more often, and the day will come when Captain Willoughby Williams will be a guest at your wedding."

He coughed and spluttered as he realised his listener's face was bright with a flush.

"Well, I never did! How are you going to manage that? If I can't stop him fishing, I can't see how you will do it."

"Never fear, my dear young lady. I have my ways. I have my ways."

Three weeks later to the day Lizzie Slocum stepped into the parlour of the White Horses and asked for Captain Willoughby Williams by name. He was, as usual, spending some time resting after a very heavy meal. His host awoke him and informed him of his visitor's presence. The Captain rose from the chair before his eyes were open, and he bowed – albeit in the wrong direction, for Lizzie Slocum stood behind his chair. The Captain slowly surveyed the room for his guest, and, finding where she was, bowed again and ushered her to a chair on the other side of the fireplace.

"And to what do I owe a visit from you, my dear?"

Secretly, he hoped it was not another invitation to be at the Slocums' for a meal. His tummy fair rumbled at the thought of the last small supper, which had sent him to bed hungry. Having worked up his usual appetite, he had had it shipwrecked at the Slocums' table.

"I've come to tell you that Donald is up to his tricks again, Captain."

"Oh, why, yes, my dear. I made you a little promise that I would do something about that, didn't I? Well, when exactly is this little fishing trip to be?"

"Tomorrow night is what he told me. And I think it must be with the rector again, for he said the boat was full."

"Did he say that, my dear? How very interesting!" There was a long pause and, then, the Captain said slowly, "Supposing you and I take a little walk down to the harbour at about the time the boat comes home again? I think my little idea will work quite well: Donald will lose his love for fishing, and you will have your man safe and sound."

Tuesday night was bright with stars, and a moon climbed slowly up from the sea to hang for some time low on the horizon. In the shadows of the harbour buildings, the Captain stood quietly talking to Lizzie Slocum and the Sergeant. The Captain looked at his watch.

"I would say they have been out for an hour and a half, for it's just half past ten."

"I told my dad and mum that I had been invited to join you for dinner at the White Horses, Captain, so I had better not be too late. What's my being here got to do with your little plan anyway?"

"Oh, there's just a very little part for you to play, my dear. Just bide with us a little longer and you will see." Then, turning to Sergeant Sigrose, the Captain asked, "Are the others in place?"

"Yes, sir. I can just see their horses breathing over there in the shadow."

All this was a surprise to Lizzie, and she began to feel that she was part of a plan she didn't understand at all. Who were these 'others', and what had they to do with her Donald and his fishing? Before she could ask any more questions, she heard a whistle from further down the harbour. Then the Captain turned and told her her special part in the plan.

"I want you to step out on to the quayside, my dear, and, as the boat comes in under the steps, just call out to Donald that he is wanted urgently at home. You don't have to say why; just make it sound urgent, and then hurry off up the hill and let him follow. I promise you, my dear, he will come to no harm."

Harm! Whatever was this? She thought she was taking part in a little fun. Now she felt there was something sinister. This little request filled her with foreboding.

The Captain gently pushed her forward and said, "Now – tell him now, quickly!"

She was frightened and confused but willing to fulfil her part.

Almost a scream came out as she called over the harbour wall to the boat below: "Donald, you're wanted at home. Do come quickly!"

Donald leaped from the prow of the small boat. He looked round at the rector and bid a hasty goodnight, then raced up the steep steps. Lizzie was nowhere in sight when he reached the top, so he called after her. She did not answer – indeed, she could not, for she had been pulled into the shadows and her mouth was covered by a gloved hand. She went limp when she saw the King's men come out from the shadows. Each man grabbed a fisherman as he appeared at the top of the steps. A tall officer grasped the prize of the night – the rector.

There was no getting away this time – no excusing themselves with humour or a hasty disguising of their contraband. They had been caught red-handed, betrayed into the hands of the law. A cask of brandy, a box of tea, several rolls of cloth, all were confiscated as the parish councillors filed along the quay. Only Donald ran into the night, free. He knew not what to do.

If he returned, he would be caught; if he did not, he felt

himself a part of the betrayal. It was his girl who had set the trap. Surely he would be thought a part of the plan. In confusion, he made his way up the hill. He knew before he arrived home that there was no emergency. His parents wondered what he was doing at their door. He lived over his workplace at the draper's shop. After telling what he had seen, he made his sad way back to the shop and watched from the safety of his upper window as a group of horse riders clattered up the hill and into the night.

He was not alone in finding sleep impossible that night. Lizzie Slocum crept in at the back door of her home and made her way to bed terrified at what had happened. She felt like Judas himself. If Donald escaped capture with the others, he would certainly be lost to her for ever. Who would want to marry a Judas, even with as pretty a face as Lizzie was supposed to have?

CHAPTER SEVENTEEN

The Trial Begins

Lower Penzle was in an uproar. Its leading citizens were in the hands of the law. Many had had their suspicions, and some had known for sure what had been going on for a whole year or more since the new rector had come to their parish church. They all knew why the King's officer was stationed at the White Horses with his sergeant. Many had laughed at the fumbling attempts they had made to capture the mysterious smugglers, often referring to the whole thing as if it were someone trying to lay a ghost. But now the whole thing was out in the open. They all knew the rector well enough to expect him to accept any blame or guilt that would be apportioned, but none knew quite how to greet him when, with the rest of his parish councillors, he was released on bail and allowed to carry on his duties.

The Reverend John Trevethin was first summoned to see the Bishop. The interview was not a lengthy one. John was ushered into the study of His Lordship, and he made a formal statement that he would be defending himself at the trial but would prefer to say nothing until the case was heard. His Lordship, who knew both John and his late father very well, expressed his strong disapproval of anything that smacked of scandal and said he hoped that John's good name would be cleared of any trace of guilt.

The interview over, John made his way back to prepare for the great day of reckoning. He had no doubt that Sir Richard Crendon would have a top man from the King's Bench to try the case. It was just the kind of publicity Sir Richard would enjoy. What was difficult for the villagers to appreciate was the cool way in which every man of the parish council approached the whole affair. Under the strong influence of their rector, each man kept his own mouth closed and awaited the day. They had run their risky path knowing full well its almost certain end. Now that that end had been reached, they seemed ready to accept the consequences.

Several weeks went past before a suitable date for the King's judge to attend a special court session at Crendon Hall arrived. Those weeks were busy ones for the defendants as well as those preparing the case for the Crown. Each week John Trevethin preached from his pulpit with almost an impish glee about him. He confessed to old Joseph Trenbeath his relish for the case as the time neared. The final parish-council meeting was solemn, with sincere prayer and serious words from the rector and the chairman. Old Joseph fair shone as he expressed his confidence in the rector. They parted to make their way to Crendon Hall for their court appearance at the time appointed.

The clock struck ten in the long dining room. The table was set now with decanter and glasses for each seated dignitary, and on the empty side of the table was laid Sir Richard's family Bible. Its brass clasps shone in the light of the fine fire which burned in the hearth. A gavel was brought down upon hard wood and the court was called to order. Then the clerk announced that this was an extraordinary court session called by order of His Majesty's judge. The wigged and robed judge looked every inch his position, and, with a voice to match, he announced who was representing the Crown. The subdued note in his voice did not betray the excitement everyone in the room was feeling. Captain Willoughby Williams, outside in the hallway, strained to hear each sentence uttered by the dignified voice. He coughed nervously as he prepared himself for the great moment when he would describe the daring exploits that had brought these wicked villains to justice. Sir Richard sat alongside the Judge as a magistrate of the local court, confident that this lawbreaking group, including its leader, was bound for prison, with heavy fines.

In the silence that followed the opening of the proceedings, only the rustle of papers could be heard. Then the prosecution's evidence was stated. The case seemed so clear-cut that it appeared hardly necessary to call the witnesses. Sir Richard listened and rubbed his hands together under the table. This he was enjoying.

The case began with a statement about the views expressed by the rector in his public pronouncement on the subject of taxes. No one could deny that all the evidence offered by the prosecution pointed to a strong motive.

Then came the long statements by Willoughby Williams. As the morning dragged on, his long account of each attempt to catch the smugglers and their tricks to cover their tracks was laid out before the court. Unfortunately for the Captain, his manner and the number of his failures only emphasised the fact that he had been less than efficient at his task. But, with a final flourish, he redeemed his position as he turned to the accused and described how they had been caught red-handed on the night of their arrest. The Captain concluded his evidence and sat down.

The prosecuting counsel closed his case, and the court adjourned for lunch. As Sir Richard's dining room was being used as the court, the Judge, and those entertaining him, left the house and made for the Coach and Horses Inn. There they ate with relish and discussed with candour the chances of the case. There was no doubt as to the guilt of the accused men, and it now rested with the King's judge to decide the sentence worthy of such a crime against His Majesty. But the Judge's words as they finished their lunch were somewhat prophetic:

"Maybe we should not count our chickens before they are hatched, gentlemen. I have seen watertight cases like this fall apart before, and, while I do not see any loophole that our friends can crawl through, one never can tell – one never can tell!"

CHAPTER EIGHTEEN

The Chickens Begin to Hatch

The afternoon session began with the announcement that there was no lawyer for the defence. The Rector of Lower Penzle had chosen to put the case for the defendants himself.

"Do you think you have made a wise choice, Reverend, sir?" asked the Judge. "I am quite prepared to accept a late submission, if you care to change your mind and call a lawyer to defend your case."

"Your Honour, I am quite happy to defend the good men who stand accused this day. Neither they nor I are guilty either of defrauding His Majesty or of bringing the law into disrepute. I beg to submit the case for the defence."

"You are within your rights so to do, sir. Pray proceed."

With this permission granted, the rector stood forward and laid his papers before him. He had never enjoyed even preaching as much as he was enjoying this moment.

"Just over one year ago, Your Honour, I was instituted Rector of Lower Penzle. Being a bachelor, and entering a house not already furnished, I attempted to purchase what I required from local merchants. I soon discovered that such purchases cost a great deal more in Lower Penzle than they would in London. Indeed, as I surveyed my bills, I was astonished to discover that the taxes for such goods were exactly double what they are in other parts of the country. I have a complete list of the prices and taxes charged on those goods."

He held a small sheaf of papers in his hand for all to see.

"On investigation, I discovered that these taxes were not the tax revenues set by His Majesty's tax officers, but an amount decided arbitrarily by the local tax collector and imposed with some rigour upon the whole community of Crendon Bywater and its outlying villages and towns. My investigations led me to discover that no steps have been taken by the higher authorities to correct this state of affairs, although representation has been made from time to time both at Truro and Bristol. Such representations have been overruled or prevented."

It was evident that Sir Richard Crendon was not at all comfortable. He had suddenly developed a cough. Such was his indignation that he once burst in on the proceedings to object that the statements being made had little or no bearing upon the guilt or innocence of the defendants.

"You will kindly leave such decisions to me," stated the Judge with a firmness that caused Sir Richard to apologise with a "Quite so, Your Honour, quite so!"

The rector continued. His evidence gradually built up to quite a case against the unjust taxes. His father's position as a tax collector was well known to the Judge, and the rector's knowledge of the laws of the land showed as he placed each fact before the court. At last, he brought his defence to its climax.

"I wish to state without excuse that the members of my parish council and I have engaged in an act of smuggling, but we have not at any time robbed His Majesty of one penny in taxes due to him."

With this statement he sat down, much to the amazement of the whole company. It seemed that he had admitted guilt for them all, and the Judge had but to pass sentence.

However, the Judge picked up the rector's last statement, and he asked the prosecution if it wished to cross-examine.

"Indeed we do, Your Honour."

"You may proceed."

The counsel for the Crown stepped forward and called for the rector to enter the witness box, which on this occasion was but a small table set on the Judge's left-hand side. The rector stepped forward and, after taking the oath on the heavy Crendon family Bible held before him, stood waiting.

The prosecuting counsel took his time.

"You are, sir, the Rector of Lower Penzle?" He addressed the rector without looking up.

"I am that, by appointment of the Bishop of Truro."

"You preached, as has been stated, on the subject of taxes."

"I brought such subjects into my sermons, yes."

"You readily admit that you did more than preach against taxes."

"If you mean by that, that I engaged in acts of smuggling to evade unjust taxes, the answer is yes!"

"If you readily admit to such acts of smuggling, then you are admitting to defrauding His Majesty of the taxes due to him."

"The answer to this accusation is an unequivocal no, sir."

"Would you kindly explain, sir, how you can evade the paying of taxes by the act of smuggling on the one hand, and not rob the King on the other?"

"Sir, I wish to submit as evidence of this a ledger which has been carefully kept by my parish clerk. This plainly states that the value of goods taken from the *Sea Winkle* comes to exactly half the total tax charged by the taxing officer at Crendon Bywater. If we paid, as we did, the amount demanded of us by the taxing officer, and this amount was the full amount of tax due to His Majesty, how, then, can we have robbed the King of his just revenue?"

The Judge adjusted his spectacles and interjected a question: "Reverend sir, are you again suggesting that the amount of tax taken by the taxing officer was double what it should have been?"

"I am that, sir!"

"I wish to adjourn the court so that I may inspect the evidence of this ledger. The court is adjourned and will reconvene in one half-hour."

Sir Richard Crendon was livid. As he approached the Judge, he could hardly control himself.

"Your Honour, this evidence has nothing to do with this case. If every Tom, Dick and Harry can decide what taxes he should pay, where will His Majesty's authority be?"

"I think we had better inspect this evidence, Sir Richard. It may throw light on the dishonesty of the rogue parson we have before us."

Though he said this with tongue-in-cheek, Sir Richard caught the words 'rogue parson' and felt a little relieved. If this was the opinion of the Judge, then this evidence would be treated with suspicion and may not be allowed.

The Judge inspected the ledger carefully, and, with the help of the rector's explanation, saw that detailed accounts had indeed been kept of every smuggling foray and every yard of cloth and barrel of spirits that had been taxed at Crendon Bywater.

When the court resumed, the Judge himself opened the questioning.

Addressing himself to the rector, he asked, "What is the amount of tax on a barrel of spirits, sir?"

"Half a guinea, sir."

"Then, why do you have one whole guinea charged on every barrel imported through Crendon Bywater?"

"Because that is the amount charged by the tax collector at Crendon Bywater, Your Honour."

"Then, by your submission, the number of barrels shipped to Lower Penzle is ten, and the number passing through the tax collector at Crendon Bywater is ten."

"That is correct, Your Honour. We have accounts with the spirits company and pay for them direct. Only the tax is paid at Crendon Bywater."

"Then, sir, the tax you paid on these twenty barrels is ten whole guineas?"

"That is correct, Your Honour."

"Then, would someone pray tell me how you have robbed His Majesty of any tax?"

The counsel for the Crown rose to his feet.

"Your Honour, this is but one small item in a whole list of commodities that are shipped through this port. There are no accounts kept of all the items which have been taken from the *Sea Winkle* by these robbers of the King's taxes."

"I beg to submit, Your Honour, that I have here details of every item taken from the *Sea Winkle*, and the master of that vessel also has details of such items."

"Call the master of the *Sea Winkle*," requested the Judge.

The master of the *Sea Winkle* entered, bidden by the clerk, and he took his place in the witness stand in place of the rector.

The master was sworn in as a witness and stood awaiting his questioning.

"Captain Storeton, I understand that your vessel had some arrangement with the rector and his men to unload certain of its cargo at sea?"

"That is right, Your Honour. Although it is not my usual practice, it was a private arrangement on the strict understanding that an account was kept which did not in any way infringe the law."

"Come, come, good captain! Surely you know that it is illegal to unload taxable items anywhere other than through a taxing officer of His Majesty's government."

"With respect to yourself, Your Honour, I know the law very well, but we have been having some unwelcome irregularities in the Crendon Bywater port of late. This was a private arrangement to get around those difficulties. I might add, Your Honour, that I have accounts to show that we have never robbed His Majesty of the just taxes due. Only the unjust taxes have been stopped, and I have all the ship's accounts to confirm that."

"I would like to review those accounts, my dear captain, but that will not be necessary just at this moment. Let me ask one further question: how long has the 'unjust' tax, as you call it, been charged, and what proof have you that it is unjust?"

"Begging your pardon, Your Honour, every trader in the district knows that the taxes are exorbitant, but this is the first time we have taken the law into our own hands."

"I will adjourn the court for today," the Judge stated in a firm voice. "I request that during this evening I be shown the tax accounts of the Crendon Bywater tax officer and the accounts of the master of the *Sea Winkle*."

Sir Richard, already furious at suggestions made during this day's proceedings, now hurried from the room. His carriage left for the harbour. At his side was the tax collector, and during the long hours of the night the oil burned in the little office on the quayside as each account was carefully inspected to make sure all was innocent of overcharged revenue.

"We are not in any danger, my man," he assured his henchman.

But neither of them really believed this for a moment as they returned to their beds for what was left of the night.

CHAPTER NINETEEN

The Day of Reckoning

The morning dawned, bright and windy, and the sun slanted in through the dining-room windows of Crendon Hall. Everyone came with their own expectations and emotions, varying from the apprehension of Sir Richard to the exhilaration of the rector.

The clerk called the court to order at a few minutes after ten o'clock. The large grandfather clock in the corner of the dining room seemed to take longer than usual to end its array of chimes and the sonorous notes of its strike.

The Judge opened the proceedings with a review of his findings. He had examined the accounts of the *Sea Winkle* and, only that morning, the accounts of the tax officer.

"I find", he said slowly, "that everything in all the accounts is in order."

A sigh of relief was audible from Sir Richard.

"But I find also some discrepancy in the amounts mentioned. If what is shown in the tax collector's records is correct, I have to ask him why a barrel of spirits is charged at one half-guinea although we have had plainly stated that the tax charged was regularly levied at one whole guinea. Seeing that my good friend Sir Richard Crendon is seated with us this morning, may I ask him to be so good as to take the stand. His knowledge of these matters is better than that of anyone else in the room, and I am sure he has an explanation for this seeming – I say *seeming* – discrepancy."

Sir Richard coloured and stood with shaky legs. He made his way to the little table where each witness had been sworn in. The clerk laboriously lifted the great Crendon family Bible and placed it in front of the witness. Sir Richard bristled as he looked down at his own Bible.

"And what, my good man, is that supposed to be for? I am not on trial here!"

"Sir Richard, may I remind you that everyone summoned to give evidence or to be questioned here must first take the oath. This is a court of law, sir!"

"Oh, I beg your pardon, Your Honour. I was a little hasty. This whole business has me quite confused. I do not know what I am being asked, or why. I have always been loyal to the King and most zealous in my duties as a magistrate. I have done nothing other than my duty, I assure you, Your Honour."

"Quite so, Sir Richard. Your duty is not in question here. I ask you simply, why is it said that a whole guinea has been charged in tax when the tax required by the King is but a half-guinea? I am sure you have a reason for this discrepancy. If you would be good enough to explain it to the court, I would be obliged."

Sir Richard coughed. He took some time clearing his throat.

"I think there must have been a few mistakes somewhere, Your Honour. I know of no reason why more should have been asked than the law demands."

"Is that the best you can do, Sir Richard?"

The whole room gazed in amazement at this lord of the manor who seemed to be shrivelling by the minute.

"Perhaps", said the Judge, "we should question the tax officer concerned. He will no doubt know if anyone does. Call the Crendon Bywater tax collector."

The man entered, and Sir Richard was removed from his position behind the witness stand.

The man took the oath and was asked his reason for the discrepancy. What he said was like dynamite in that room already hot with excitement.

"Your Honour, I am first a tax collector for the King, and, as such, I answer you without fear of man. I am, however, also in the employ of Sir Richard Crendon, who is Inspector for His Majesty's Taxes in these parts. I have to state that there is another book, not here in the court, which bears the true record of these matters. I beg to be allowed to fetch that book. It will reveal the true nature of this case."

At the close of this brief statement, there was a sound like a cow beginning to low in its stall. Sir Richard tried to stand, but he swayed, tottered to his knees, and crumpled to the floor.

"Please assist Sir Richard, will you?" said the Judge. "I think he will need a little reviving."

The book in question was brought to the room, and the Judge spent a moment surveying its pages with the tax collector.

The Judge spoke: "Gentlemen of this court, I wish to state that I find there is no case for the defendants to answer. I am aware that smuggling is an illegal act, but I am hard put to it to know a definition of smuggling that covers the procurement of one's own property when full tax has been paid on that property. I also find that there is a case to bring against a certain Sir Richard Crendon on a charge of extortion, the evidence for which case is neither complete nor obtainable at this time. I therefore freely discharge the defendants and ask the Crown to prepare a case for a future hearing at His Majesty's pleasure on the said case of extortion. Gentlemen, I hereby adjourn this court at thirty minutes past eleven of the clock on this 10th day of December."

It might have been a cheer, and it might just have been the sudden rise in voices that everyone in the hall outside the dining room heard, but, as the doors were opened and the Judge came forth, pandemonium broke out. One after another the defendants were embraced and paraded forth out of the room to make their way home to Lower Penzle.

"You know, Joseph," said the rector as they drove home in Joseph's trap, "I am going to miss our nights of fishing, but I have a feeling Lizzie Slocum might now get her Donald – poor lad!"

THE SMUGGLER IN DISGUISE

CHAPTER ONE

A Visitor from France

If you have ever wondered how a smuggler could settle to a quiet and unadventurous life, you may cease your wondering. The Reverend John Trevethin could not settle to a quiet and unadventurous life in the parish of Lower Penzle. His preaching and pastoral duties fully occupied his working hours, and, faithful clergyman that he was, his working hours were long. But after his strange and unexpected adventures as an honest smuggler, of which my last story told, life seemed somewhat tame. Often the members of his faithful parish council would reminisce and laugh together over some memory of those days.

It was during one such meeting of these men, which had more to do with the past adventures than present parish business, that a visitor was announced by Mrs Jones, the rector's good housekeeper.

"He sounds a little strange to me, sir, but he says his business is very urgent."

His strangeness was soon apparent to all. It was the strangeness of a strong French accent. Immaculately dressed in fine brocades, he bowed in a theatrical manner and apologised for intruding into a business session of the worthy rector and his men.

"My gracious English friends, I do apologise for my arrival at such a time, but you will see that it is – what word do you use? – ah, providential that we are able to meet as a company."

The manner and content of these opening remarks left even the rector speechless. The moment of silence was broken only by the rector begging the visitor to continue.

"I am most grateful for your permission, *Monsieur le Recteur*. May I say that I have heard of your escapades as smugglers and have laughed so hard at the stories Captain Storeton has related to me."

"Oh, I see. So our worthy friend, the Captain, is our point of contact," interjected the rector.

"Ah, yes, but do forgive me for wandering on. I have come, not merely to congratulate you upon your successful adventures in this strange role, but to ask your gracious help, good gentlemen."

This address to all who were gathered had a startling effect on them. At first sight, Joseph Trenbeath, the parish-council chairman and senior of all in the room, thought this visitor was a newspaper reporter from across the Channel, or maybe some theatrical agent looking for actors to play a part in a play about smugglers, but now he noted an earnestness in the visitor's voice and manner which roused his interest. As the Frenchman addressed himself to them all, old Joseph became convinced that something serious was afoot.

"And how, my good friend, can we help you?" asked the rector, half afraid that the help he was going to ask was financial – or perhaps illegal. He too was all ears.

"You will all be acquainted with the troubles which are besetting my country just now."

"We are aware of the revolutionary forces at work there – yes, sir. Pray go on."

The rector had heard much of the bloodshed under the blade of the guillotine with its fearless operators. Was this man a revolutionary or one of the few noblemen to have escaped with his head still upon his shoulders?

"You may also have heard that a very brave Englishman has been assisting some of those caught in the jaws of this revolutionary animal."

With this statement, all knew which side the Frenchman was on and breathed a little easier. Sympathies for the revolutionaries were running lower every day in England as more French blood was running from the guillotine. Unjust laws and unequal riches seemed little excuse for such indiscriminate slaughter of men, women and even children. The almost miraculous escapes arranged and daringly carried out by an English nobleman had come to light with his recent near capture and exposure. He could no more work as he had, and it seemed the door of escape might have now been closed. Many went to meet their fate, untried and condemned, for no greater wrong than simply showing sympathy for those already imprisoned or executed.

"I come to you, gentlemen, because I think, if you are willing, you could do a service to my countrymen in distress."

"Come, come, good sir! Are you suggesting", answered the rector for them all, "that we have a part to play in another country's political upheavals? And how, anyway, could quiet, little Lower Penzle play such a part?"

"That, Reverend, sir, is just my reason for coming to you, here in this 'quiet, little Lower Penzle', as you say. Your manner of operation during your last little exercise with the British Customs gives me great hope that you could use those talents yet again to save some very precious lives that otherwise will be sacrificed to the extremists of this whole dread upheaval. If you will give me time, I would lay out my plan, but I must first have your word that you will open your mouth and put your foot in it, as I think you say."

At this there was a round of laughter, and the poor man stood, for the first time, red-faced and speechless.

"I think you mean you want us to hold our tongues," volunteered the rector, trying not to laugh their visitor into more embarrassment.

"Ah, you know what I am trying to say, good sir. Thank you! I am not quite used with your idioms."

"That's quite all right; I make the same mistakes with my

French, only your people are more polite than we are here tonight. I do apologise."

"Oh, please, please, do not say sorry. I enjoy your humour so much; and, after what I have endured these past days, a little laughter is a medicine to me. Thank you."

The hour was getting late, and one or two men were shifting about in their seats, knowing that suppers were awaiting them and their wives would be full of questions as to why a meeting which all had said would be short had been so long. The rector, sensing the mood, suggested a dismissal of all who wished to leave, and any who wished to stay could do just that. One or two made a move; and when most of the twelve had left, Timothy Wiseman (the village grocer), Joshua and young Donald Creedy were left with the rector and his visitor.

Mrs Jones brought in hot drinks for those left and, as they quietly sipped from the heavy earthenware mugs, each eyed the others in the warm lamplight of this room full of memories. What lay in store for them now, they each wondered without uttering a word for what seemed a long time. Only the sound of the long pendulum clock ticking away the minutes broke the silence of that little company.

CHAPTER TWO

A Narrow Escape

"Have you rooms at the inn?" asked the rector as he put down his mug on the tray before him and the others reached forward and did the same.

"No, no, *Monsieur le Recteur*. I did not want everyone to know that I had been in the village. I rode straight here from Crendon Bywater when I landed on the *Sea Winkle* earlier this evening. I shall return there and lodge as Captain Storeton's guest, I think."

"Come, my friend! I know not how long we shall talk, but it will be too late for you to journey there tonight. I insist that Mrs Jones puts a warming pan through one of our beds here tonight, and you can leave at what time you choose in the morning."

"That is too, too kind, Reverend, sir. It would suit me admirably. I gladly accept your kindness."

"Well, that's done, sir."

With this, the rector rose and left the room to inform Mrs Jones about their overnight guest. When he returned to the room the visitor got down to business.

"I have come to ask if you will use your skills to bring certain friends of mine ashore and into hiding for a brief time, as you no doubt did your contraband in times past. I cannot offer you payment for this task, but your reward will be to know you have saved lives. You will be asked to do no more than that, good sirs."

Each man looked into the smouldering fire as its embers died to a mere glow. Then old Joseph took the initiative and spoke of his forebears and their part in saving the lives of men in the days of Judge Jeffreys and his persecutions.

"I think", said he, "that my old grandfather would have enjoyed being here tonight."

"And what would your *grandpère* have enjoyed so much, old friend?" asked the Frenchman in such a friendly way that Joseph warmed even more to open the secrets he had shared with no man outside the smugglers' group. He rose and went to the bookshelves. His finger found the secret latch, and, before the amazed eyes of the Frenchman, those beautiful polished shelves swung easily out into the room.

"Look'ee here," said old Joseph.

The visitor walked across and peered down the winding steps that led into the cellar and thence to the tunnel which led away underground to the church. As he peered down and listened to Joseph's tale, he let out a long, low whistle.

"Messieurs, I trust we are in business. I feel in my heart that you are with me."

He had hardly spoken these seeming words of contract when there was a loud knocking at the rector's front door – no bell pulled, just a strong and loud knock. The rector called for Mrs Jones to answer the door.

"It is probably her brother-in-law from the inn, though why he should knock is a trifle strange."

It was that fact which made them all listen to Mrs Jones' conversation with the person at the door. It was not Mrs Jones' relative, and indeed, from the guttural French accent, it was obvious to all that it was no local parishioner.

The Frenchman in their midst stiffened at the sound of his countryman's voice.

"Quick!" he said. "This man is my enemy. Let me take this tunnel to your church and get away. He must not find me here or the game is up. Boy," he said, addressing Donald Creedy, "take my horse, as if it is your own, and ride it down to the church. I will find my way out to you somehow. Rector, I trust you to cover my exit, and, please, do not let this man know where I am. I feared he might come – but not so soon. Let me out, I beg you."

There was certainly no time for explanations. The visitor exited down the stairs and the bookshelves swung back into place. He would have to grope his way through the darkness, and the rector hoped no earth had fallen in the tunnel since last it was used.

Mrs Jones came in to announce this new stranger, and the rector showed Timothy, Joseph and Donald to the door.

"Goodnight, gentlemen – and Donald, my lad, watch that fine horse as you take her down the hill. I'm sure she is enjoying her new rider. She will make you a fine companion as well as a good mount."

They all echoed the rector's goodnight and went out into the darkness, past the stranger standing in the hall.

"Well, good sir, what brings you to Lower Penzle Rectory at this late hour?"

"Please excuse my intrusion, rector, but a very good friend of mine, a fellow countryman, passed this way a short time ago and some in the village said he had been asking for the rectory. I have urgent business with him, good sir, so if you can tell me of his whereabouts, I would be obliged. I am to sail for France in the morning, and I must deliver a special message to him before then."

The rector invited the man into his study and sat him down. Taking his time, he looked at the man long and earnestly and then asked him a question.

"Would you mind telling me what exactly is going on just now? First, I get a visit from a man who flees my house before telling me even his name, and then a second Frenchman, himself never introducing himself to me, wants to know where the first man has gone. Is this some kind of strange game you are playing, sir?"

"Oh, I beg your pardon, my good padre. Let me introduce myself. I am Pierre Latreque, of the People's Court of the French Republique. I do not wish to appear rude, sir, but my business is urgent. I must know where my friend has gone and how I might catch him. It is a matter of life and death, I assure you."

The rector thought that it might easily be a matter of death, if he had interpreted his first visitor's fears correctly. Had he now got through the tunnel and away? How could this man be stalled longer?

"Well, now, you say this friend of yours came here. May I ask where he came from?"

"He came on the morning boat, as did I. He must return with me on tomorrow morning's boat. Do you know where he went? You must surely know how long he has been gone."

The man's manner would have given the rector's sensitive mind enough suspicion of evil intent, even if his first visitor had not expressed his fears.

"Well, good sir, I cannot tell you where your friend has gone, but I would guess that if you are both to take that morning boat, he has probably taken the high road for Crendon Bywater. In fact, now that I think of it, he did say something about the captain of the *Sea Winkle* and his rooms at the Terrapin Inn. You might try there. But it seems strange that you did not pass him on your way here, if indeed he took the high road to the east. May I suggest you try there first. Apart from that, I know not how to help you. I would if I could. But what I can offer you is a hot drink. Why don't you take your coat off and warm yourself on this cold night? You have a brisk and breezy ride ahead of you."

"Really, sir, you are very kind, but my business requires haste, and if your information proves false, I must search elsewhere."

"*False* is a rather hard word, sir. Why might I be offering you false information?"

"I ask your pardon, Monsieur. I did not mean that as a

reflection against anything you have said, but you know so little of my friend's whereabouts that I may, indeed, have much searching to do before morning."

This said, the Frenchman rose to his feet. He was well over six feet tall and even the taller-than-average rector seemed short by his side. The rector felt a little apprehensive of this man, to say the least, and he bade his visitor goodnight with genuine fear that he might well catch up with the first man before morning. Would the rector or any of his men ever see or hear from their earlier visitor again? He closed the door slowly as he heard the scurry of hooves down the hill past the church. Where, just now, was their friend of the aristocrats? How could he have held his second caller longer? He felt such sympathy with the first visitor and such antipathy towards the second.

CHAPTER THREE

Sailing in Disguise

The rector returned to his study, but, before he was seated, he heard the clatter of hooves. He rose quickly and opened the door before the horseman had alighted. He saw his first visitor of that evening dismount, and he hurried out into the cold night to usher him to the stables at the rear of the rectory.

"So, good sir, you eluded your friend. Will you still stay the night with us?"

The Frenchman spat as he spoke: "Excuse me, *Monsieur le Recteur*, this man is no friend of mine, nor of the French people. He is a perpetrator of the foul deeds that are leading our nation to anarchy and utterly needless bloodshed. I trust you not to betray me to him."

This was an interesting request. It provoked the rector to ask his friend from across the Channel, "What makes you think I did not? Maybe he is just now returning to catch you red-handed and take you with him on tomorrow morning's sailing."

"But, Monsieur, you would have not shared with me your secret tunnel and sent that dear boy to bring me back here if that was your game. No, no, I trust you, and I believe you have chosen which side you are on, whatever may be your politics."

"Oh, my unnamed friend, you need have no fear of my politics in this affair. I have little sympathy with the revolutionaries. They have already lost the ear of most Englishmen by their methods – apart from the colour of their politics."

The two men set the horse in the stall and walked carefully in the darkness to the rear entrance of the house. Mrs Jones turned suddenly as they entered her kitchen.

"Why, bless you, sir! You gave me a start. I had no idea you were at the back of the house. And I see our friend has returned to take up a nice warm bed. Shall I serve you another drink, sir?"

"I think not, Mrs Jones, unless you, sir, would care for more before we retire. Mrs Jones, we shall be leaving at a very early hour, and I think I may be away for a couple of days, upcountry. I will not say more than that, for you may well have questions asked you, and I do not want you to say anything more than that I have gone upcountry."

"Will you require a good breakfast, then?"

"Yes, we will eat at five; and what say you to a few sandwiches in cloth for us both? Would you wrap them separately? I think that will do. You are welcome to take your days away, if you wish. I am not expecting any church business to come this way. If there should be such, Joshua will know what to do. Goodnight – God give you a restful one."

"Goodnight, gentlemen. You will find clean linen on your beds and hot water on the stands. I hope you will be comfortable, sir. Have a good journey tomorrow."

She addressed the Frenchman as she said this, and he cast a quick glance at the rector. Had he already discussed 'tomorrow' with his good housekeeper?

"Oh, no," replied the rector when his visitor plied him with this question. "Mrs Jones is a very canny woman; she puts two and two together and always gets her sums right. Now we have to discuss tomorrow ourselves, for I have a plan that I think may be a little unorthodox, but it will get you where you want to go, if I read you aright. I suspect that you, too, wish to sail on that boat tomorrow."

"Yes," replied the visitor, "I must be in Paris tomorrow evening, and the good Captain Storeton has promised he will get me there if I can make the harbour before he sails. But how can I get on board unobserved by Monsieur Latreque? He will keep watch till the ropes are cast off, and I suspect he will not be alone in his vigil."

"Friend, first share with me your name, and as we climb the stair I will tell you my plan for the morning."

"My name is Jack Dart – at least, that is what I am known as. My family name is that of an old French family. Already my uncle has suffered the penalty for his sympathies, and my brother is at this very moment in the Bastille. Henry has been incarcerated these past four years, and I marvel that I have not already seen his head roll into the wretched basket of the guillotine. He has refused to escape more than once that others might be got out; but if I could give my life for his, I would see him released. Oh, good sir, you know not the half of what is happening in the corruption of what these revolutionaries say is the new day for France. It is more like an old nightmare."

"Jack, I feel in my bones that our friendship is going to be a long one. I do not see you losing your life just yet a while. Let's think very carefully on this present difficulty. Here is my plan. . . ."

With this, they turned into the visitor's bedroom, and, lowering their heads under the beam that ran up diagonally across the entrance to the room, they sat together on the edge of the white counterpane. Jack's eyes opened wider again as he saw, not into a secret tunnel, but into a wardrobe that stood on the outside wall of the room. Here, before his eyes, were dresses and suits of every description.

'What in the world', he thought, 'is a veritable theatrical wardrobe doing here in the rectory of a good Anglican priest?'

The rector answered his unasked question with a chuckle.

"I see you are surprised? You need not be. I inherited this array from my parents. My father was somewhat of an actor before he turned to the ways of God. I know that he originally intended to become a priest, but his age was against him, and I suppose you could say that I fulfilled his dream. He was able to see me ordained before his departure, and no father could have been more happy. I think he was a little proud of me too. But, Jack, we are not here to recall my family history. These clothes have been aired but little since those days. I have fun at Christmas with my guests, but otherwise they are here gathering dust. Tomorrow they shall see the light of day, methinks, and you and I will sail together on the *Sea Winkle* as two very different people.'

They slept well and woke early. Mrs Jones had breakfast ready, and they ate a hearty meal before riding together down into the village. Their first call was to awaken Donald Creedy. He was already half dressed when they rattled softly at his upper window with small pebbles. Donald peered down at his early visitors and then hurried to open the shop door to them, for he lived above the draper's establishment where he earned his living.

'Rector, what ails you? Is there something more I can do for our French visitor?'

'Yes, Donald, my lad, you can get some breakfast inside you and meet us at Timothy Wiseman's grocery store. Be sharp. We have little time. Oh, leave a note for your employer that the rector required you to take an urgent message to Crendon Bywater, for that's where we are all off to. But not another word! Hurry, lad, hurry.'

The door closed and the two men took the back lane behind the shops with their horses. They eventually tied them at the rear of Timothy's warehouse. Lights were burning and Timothy soon answered their knock.

'Rector! Come in, come in. What brings you at this early hour? And our French friend – I thought you, sir, were safely sleeping at the Terrapin before your journey back to your own country.'

"No, Timothy, Jack stayed the night with me. But, what is more important, we must catch that morning boat and we have precious little time to get there."

"Oh, you have plenty of time to ride to Crendon, and the morning is a fair one."

"Ah," said the rector, "that is where you are wrong, good Timothy, my friend. We are going in your cart, and that will cut our time, or, shall I say, prolong our ride."

"But why take a trundling old cart when you can ride there in half the time on your horses?"

"Well," answered the rector, "we shall be taking with us a large basket, if you can lend me one, and I shall require some of your good lady's dishes."

"Timothy, friend," said the Frenchman, "I do not cease to wonder at *Monsieur le Recteur*. He has the most fantastic plan. If it works, we are safe; if it doesn't, he will be the laughing stock of every parish from here to London."

Timothy Wiseman's cart drew up at the quayside. On it was seated a young driver who anyone could have recognised as Donald Creedy of the Lower Penzle draper's store. But the tall, well-built woman at his side in black crêpe and heavy travelling shawl was a complete stranger.

CHAPTER FOUR

Dishes for Notre Dame

Standing on deck were most of the passengers and Captain Storeton. He and one other were looking beyond the few who gathered on the quayside before the ship sailed. Crew members were chatting with their shore colleagues, awaiting the order to cast off. Children played games around harassed carters, whose waggons had just completed their unloading and who were about to load the barrels and bales standing on the quayside. None paid too much attention to the small cart and its two riders. Donald got down and handed the reins to his passenger to hold while he went aboard and asked for help with luggage. It was a very large basket, and the lady was most attentive as this obviously very heavy container was carried up the gangplank.

Suddenly, Donald felt a hand grip his shoulder.

"My friend, we meet again!"

Donald turned and coloured a little when he realised he was looking at the second visitor at the rectory of last evening. He regained his composure and, after a moment of hesitation, apologised that he had not recognised his acquaintance.

"Oh, that is all right, *mon ami*. We met but for a moment last evening. But tell me: did you see my French colleague? I am at a loss to know what can be detaining him. The good captain here is anxious to leave on time, and I am just as anxious that we do not miss each other."

Donald looked at the stranger and answered as easily as he could: "Oh, yes, I saw your friend. He came to the rectory earlier in the evening and left rather hurriedly. I think he must be in Crendon. It would not take him long to get here, even if he spent the night at the White Horses."

"The White Horses?" asked the Frenchman. "Did he spend the night there? Is that not the inn I enquired at in Lower Penzle?"

"Oh, I'm only suggesting that is a possibility. I have no idea where he spent the night. But surely if he returned here last night, you would have met with him by now?"

Before the Frenchman could answer Donald's question, the Captain tapped his passenger's arm.

"I'm afraid we are going to have to leave, whether or not your friend is on board. I must catch the tide, and it's running pretty strong already."

"All right, Captain, but I leave a mystified man. Jack Dart was as keen to be here as I. It is unlike that upper-class brat to miss the boat."

"Cast off!" said the Captain quietly to his mate.

"Cast off fore and aft," shouted the mate to his men.

The *Sea Winkle* lifted a little as the ropes released her from the quayside, and the sails, already stretched taut in the morning breeze coming offshore, propelled her out into the centre of the harbour stream. She looked a pretty sight, old as she was, headed out to bear south and then due east up the Channel for the narrow crossing higher up the coast in sheltered water on her way to France.

The voyage was completely uneventful. Some passengers stayed much of the early part of it on deck, but a keen Atlantic wind sped the little ship up the Channel and chased many of its passengers to what warmth there was below decks.

In Captain Storeton's cabin was a rare sight indeed: a lady taking tea and quietly chatting to the Captain as he came and went from his duties. She never ventured once on deck – not, that is, until the ship was tied up again at its French destination.

An angry Pierre Latreque brushed past his disembarking fellow passengers on to the shore of his homeland. He was angry on two accounts: he had missed his quarry, and he had torn his hose on a wretched basket, which was being joggled down the gangway when he was wanting to hurry past. If he had been a little more attentive, he might have heard a snigger from the basket. But then, who would have expected a basket of carefully packed dishes to snigger?

The angry Frenchman made his way to a waiting carriage, and the tall lady in black crêpe directed four men to carry her precious dishes carefully into a warehouse. She waited until she was sure she was alone, and then she removed the leather straps from their buckles.

She carefully took each shallow pile of dishes from its resting place, pulled back the soft cloths upon which they rested, lifted a board, and there was Jack Dart. The strong arms of the lady in black lifted the stiff-limbed Frenchman from his resting place, and, as the two laughed together, the lady stripped off her coat and removed her wig. After carefully replacing the dishes, cloths and board in as safe a manner as time would allow, the rector and Jack carried the much lighter luggage back to the *Sea Winkle* and into Captain Storeton's cabin. It seemed as though the plan had worked. Certainly, the carriage was gone and no Pierre was there to view the transformation that had taken place.

Assuring the Captain that he would be back in recognisable form before he sailed again, the rector left on foot with Jack Dart to find some horses for the brisk ride to Paris and a special meeting with their friends at Notre Dame.

CHAPTER FIVE

The First Delivery

The shadows cast by the flickering oil lamps in Notre Dame's great vaulted crypt made it difficult for the rector to distinguish those he was meeting. They each mumbled a French greeting, and it was during those brief introductions that the keen ear of the rector noted some female voices among the priestly figures, and he realised that some were dressed in nuns' habits.

This was a meeting in the vaults beneath Notre Dame organised by men and women interested in the rescue of those caught or about to be caught in the web of events which had brought so many victims to the guillotine.

The rector was thanked for his part in bringing Jack Dart back to them all in safety. His being there, surprise though it was to them, made him realise that Jack's visit to England and Lower Penzle had been carefully planned and that he was well known, by name if not personally. The voice that spoke was that of a woman, though the garb she wore was that of a priest. The rector had already made it clear that his French was good enough for him not to need a translator, and, as he listened to the request that was being made, he realised that there was little chance now of his refusal. He was a vital part of this rescue plan, with all its dangers.

The plan thus revealed, he made his way on horseback with a new companion and found the *Sea Winkle* ready for departure. At the gangplank, however, there was the unwelcome presence of a revolutionary guard who was checking every passenger as he or she embarked. The Captain stood at the head of the gangplank and gave any confirmation that was necessary for each passenger known to him to come on board. When the rector appeared with his new companion, the guard asked for papers. For a moment the rector hesitated to speak, but then, with his usual bold manner recovered, he called to Captain Storeton and asked for confirmation of his identity. Without hesitation the Captain called a welcome, and he was so effusive in that welcome that the guard not only waved the rector of Lower Penzle on board, but his companion as well.

Stretched out in the cabin, the weary rector introduced the newcomer to Captain Storeton. The Captain rose to his feet and offered his hand to this person in priestly garb. In fact, the young woman who hid beneath clerical attire was almost at the point of exhaustion. She began softly to sob.

"Now, now, my young friend, you must not give way to all you feel just yet. We are by no means safely in England. You must change as quickly as you can. If the good captain will allow the use of his cabin, you must assume womanly dress again. I have in this basket clothing suitable for you, and it would be as well if you changed immediately."

No sooner had John Trevethin, the worthy Rector of Lower Penzle, uttered his piece than the sound of a commotion was heard upon the quay. Looking through the small cabin window, the Captain could just discern the tall figure of Pierre Latreque striding towards the boat from his carriage.

"There is not a moment to lose, my dear. We will delay our good Pierre as long as we can, but you must be dressed in this black crêpe before he enters this cabin."

Gathering herself together emotionally, the young woman hardly waited for the cabin doors to close before she ripped her cassock off and slipped into the womanly attire of someone quite a bit taller than she. There was a knock at the door.

"I think you met this lady yesterday on the trip over from England," said the Captain as he introduced Mrs Sarah Ryan. "I rather fear that Mrs Ryan is a little upset at the moment. She has just returned from Paris, where she was quite unprepared for the sights she saw around the guillotine. I have done my best to comfort the dear lady, but I fear she will not again want to bring her dishes for sale in your fine country, Mr Latreque."

Pierre Latreque was both embarrassed and infuriated by these remarks, but the presence of a lady so genuinely distraught prevented him from railing against the Captain. The best he could say was that he hoped Mrs Ryan would have a good crossing and that, in spite of the difficulties his country was passing through, he trusted she would indeed come back and see a fairer France. With these words he bowed and took his leave of the tearful lady. Had he looked a little closer, he might have asked why a priest's robe and cross should have been in the cabin with a lady, but his confusion caused him to leave as hurriedly as he had come. He was obviously intent on finding whoever it was who had escaped that day from Paris and made for the port.

As he made a scan of the deck, he saw his man. His informant had said 'a person disguised as a priest', and there at the rail of the ship, casually looking out to sea, was indeed a priest. Pierre Latreque marched across the deck and, standing near enough to speak softly, he breathed a request for the man to turn and face him. The priest did not turn around. Latreque spoke louder, and this time there was no avoiding a confrontation. The priest turned and faced his questioner, but there was no fear or panic on the face of this man. It was Monsieur Latreque who paled, for there before his surprised gaze was the Rector of Lower Penzle. No escapee from the Bastille, no disguised runaway from the guillotine, but the smiling face of a worthy and genuine English rector.

"You are obviously still looking for your friend," said the rector.

"I – I don't quite understand, *Monsieur le Recteur*. I had no idea you were here."

"Oh, but my dear sir, I came over on the boat at the same time as yourself, just yesterday morning. I am surprised that you did not see me. I was much in conversation with Captain Storeton and more than interested that your friend had not turned up. Have you really not traced his whereabouts? I will be most interested to hear whether or not you meet up. I have yet to be formally introduced to him. His visit was so hurried and the whole of that night's meetings are surrounded with an air of mystery. Indeed, good sir, it was your visit and his that inspired me to make this trip and see for myself the France I knew in my college days. I fear I did not like what I saw. I am sorry to say it, but I did not like what I saw."

"Quite, quite," said a very embarrassed and mystified Pierre Latreque as he bowed and excused himself.

Captain Storeton gave the orders and the mate shouted across the decks. The old ship creaked, and above the heads of those on board the sails flapped as they fell from the yards to catch what breeze there was. Slowly the *Sea Winkle* eased her way from the quay and out into the swells of the Channel. Pierre Latreque stood, his hand on the door of his coach, for a long, long while as he watched the little coastal ship go out into the jumble of ships and boats that stood at anchor.

"I must follow that man and keep a close watch on his movements. If I'm not mistaken, we have on our hands another Englishman who seeks to build a bridge from the Bastille to Britain." With those words spoken under his breath, he looked at his coachman and ordered him to get him back to Paris. Inside the coach he slapped his hand on his knee and said aloud to himself with some vehemence, "Why cannot these English dogs stay in their own kennels. The day will come when their barking will be for their own aristocracy as it hangs from England's own revolutionary gallows.

At the rail of the ship, the rector handed his charge to Captain Storeton's care to be entertained at the Terrapin Inn until the day of the Plymouth coach with connections for London and her friends awaiting her there.

CHAPTER SIX

The Cat and the Mouse

Monsieur Latreque arrived at his house in the centre of Paris, annoyed and frustrated. Not only had his victim eluded him, but his visit to England had been counterproductive. He had aroused the interest of the Rector of Lower Penzle and probably gained for his enemies a friend. Why had this Anglican rector travelled all the way to France, and how had Latreque not seen him on the journey as he returned from England? He ate his meal with no pleasure and slept only fitfully. He awoke at an early hour, and after a meeting with the Revolutionary Committee he agreed to return to England to watch this new friend of the aristocracy of his homeland.

A few days later he completed the westerly crossing again in the *Sea Winkle*, but, unknown to him, he was accompanied by a warning letter handed to Captain Storeton for his friend the rector. Jack Dart had kept close checks on his enemy and had scribbled a hasty warning to the Rector of Lower Penzle in order that he might not be caught in any kind of trap. It was a well-needed warning, for Pierre Latreque was like a cat hunting a mouse. He meant to get the rector, however much time and money it cost him.

His stay at the Terrapin Inn was prolonged. He made careful enquiries as to how and by whom the smugglers' gang of past days, led by the rector, had been trapped and apprehended.

The landlord of the Terrapin Inn was voluble in telling the tale. He laid great emphasis on the part played by the lord of the manor, and how the rector turned the tables on Sir Richard Crendon of Crendon Hall.

Pierre set off as soon as it was a respectable hour to call on this gentleman. He was admitted into the study of Sir Richard and, after a brief introduction, stated that he would like to discuss the activities of a certain Reverend John Trevethin. He watched carefully and noted with some pleasure that Sir Richard flushed as the name was mentioned.

"The man is not fit to occupy his position; he's not even a true man of the Church, sir," said Sir Richard, without troubling to find out whether he was speaking to a friend or an enemy of the rector.

"Sir Richard, do I detect that you would be happy to assist me in stopping this renegade clergyman from getting involved in another smuggling escapade?"

"Another smuggling escapade? I don't understand, sir. I would do a great deal to get that man removed from his parish, if I could. He has caused me the greatest humiliation of my life and made me the laughing stock of my own estate. I would like nothing better than to assist you, if it would lead to the downfall of that man!"

Sir Richard's vehement outburst ended with a growl of deep disgust. He settled back in his chair and glowered into the fire.

"Sir Richard, I think you can assist me. This might lead to a benefit for yourself as well as the French people."

"Oh, I don't know anything about your French people, or what they have to do with that wretched rector fellow, but tell me what it is you want of me."

The testiness of Sir Richard showed in his movements as much as his voice. He had been deeply wounded by the reversal of the case against the smugglers, and it had all been the rector's fault. Sir Richard himself had in the end only just escaped a prison sentence, and he had been removed from his former post as His Majesty's tax inspector. He was glad to assist in anything to bring down the rector from his pulpit and position of respect. He became furious at every mention of this man's name. He was determined that he would one day get even with him; and if this was the day, he would take every advantage of it.

Together Pierre Latreque and Sir Richard made their plans. They talked of the rector's possible involvement in the rescue of aristocrats from across the Channel.

"I think I heard from the innkeeper at the Terrapin that the officer who made the final capture of the smugglers is now resident in Lower Penzle."

Latreque had all the details, and in his mind the plan of attack.

"Oh," said Sir Richard, "that man is a fool, and his sergeant is a double fool."

"But is it not true that he caught the smugglers?" Latreque asked.

"Oh yes, you could say that, but he took his time about it."

"I was thinking", mused the Frenchman, "he might be able to keep an eye on the rector and do it without arousing suspicion."

"Well, he certainly has time. He has all the time in the world. He spends every hour of his retirement either quaffing ale at the White Horses or visiting widows who accept his flatteries while he accepts their pastries. Yes, you could do worse than employ that foolhardy, retired, oversized barrel of appetite."

Latreque laughed out loud as he listened to Sir Richard's description of an officer of the King of England. But he had his plan settled, so he took his leave of Sir Richard and made his way back to the Terrapin Inn. There he made enquiries of anyone going to Lower Penzle that night. He found a man and scribbled a note.

The next day at four thirty in the afternoon, Captain Willoughby Winton Williams arrived and asked for Monsieur Pierre Latreque.

"The gentleman is expecting me," he said in a pompous voice for all to hear.

Monsieur Latreque eyed his man from the other side of the parlour and didn't like what he saw: a rotund, little man in long coat and tricorn hat.

When Latreque was pointed out to him, Captain Williams marched forward with hand outstretched. Coughing and bowing, he announced his name at length.

"Captain Willoughby Winton Williams, retired officer of the King, at your service, sir. Thank you for your letter. I hurried as soon as I could get transport. I'm afraid these parts are not served well with coaches, you know."

"I would hardly think so, my dear man, but I am obliged to you for coming today. I must sail tomorrow morning and be in Paris tomorrow night, so let me get down to the business at hand. Landlord," called Latreque across the room, "bring us both drink and some food while we talk."

At the mention of a possible feast, Captain Williams removed his coat; then he took a large, clean handkerchief from his pocket and tucked it into his collar. He sat up to the table as if he were a child obeying the call to lunch.

Latreque smiled cynically. This man really was a fool, but he was a fool in the right place. Latreque set his task before the Captain.

Willoughby Winton Williams listened with some disappointment. He had imagined some intriguing journey across the Channel, an escapade in France, and all he was being asked to do was return to Lower Penzle and, once again, take up his post watching a rector who had so often outwitted and outmanoeuvred him. Was he to be of no more use than a cat watching a mouse?

Latreque waited for Captain Williams to empty his mouth of a huge bite from the meat pie that filled his plate. Mopping the gravy from his cheeks, he looked up just for a second to say he accepted the task, drank a mouthful from his tankard and spluttered out an apologetic question.

"I am honoured to serve the French Government in this way," he began with a grand sweep of the fork in his left hand, "but I might just add a little request. I do not wish to detract from the honour I feel at being asked, but" – and here he coughed a little nervous cough – "I was wondering what might be the usual honorarium for such a service to a foreign power?"

"Oh, you need have no fear, Monsieur. My government will pay you well – but only on results you achieve."

"Quite so, quite so. I was just wondering if there might be a small retaining fee?"

Latreque could see that this man, though a fool, had a wise head for his own business affairs. He threw a guinea on the table, and the Captain caught it as it rolled his way. He looked at it as though he was short-sighted, then, pocketing it, placed his fat little hand on Latreque's.

"A deal, my good sir, a deal! I only need to ask how and where I can contact your government when I have some information."

Latreque told him to leave any news he might have at the Terrapin Inn, and it would be dispatched whenever a boat was bound for the French coast. His task was to watch for anything that implicated the rector in the transportation of men or women from France via this part of the coast.

Captain Williams accepted the offer of a second helping of meat pie, and he said farewell to Latreque with his mouth still full, spurting crumbs at the Frenchman as he did so. Latreque went up to his room, and much later Captain Williams left with a carter who agreed to drop him as near to Lower Penzle as he could on his way along the high road.

It was a cold night, but Willoughby Winton Williams had a full stomach and a new gold guinea in his pocket. It had been worth his while making the journey. He was back on the job. This time the cat would catch the mouse and be paid for the trouble.

CHAPTER SEVEN

Refugees for the Rector

Of the employment of Captain Williams for his task, the rector knew nothing, and he greeted the retired soldier with the same cordiality as he always did when the gentleman attended church on Sunday morning. The Captain went to church on a fairly regular basis, knowing that he would most certainly be invited to some widow's house for a meal, either on Sunday evening or, perhaps, during the week. He was accepted as a member of the community by most, and his part in the catching of the smugglers was, if not forgotten, forgiven. He had, after all, been doing his duty as an officer of the King. Now he was a retired man, of small private means, living at the White Horses. His only hope was that his previous companion, the Sergeant, would never find him there, for now the Captain occupied the constricted attic room his sergeant had previously had. It was both cheap and sufficient, but, in spite of it being at the top of the house, it was a comedown to move from his former lodgings into those of his sergeant.

One day the Captain paid a call on the rector.

"Good morning, rector. I trust this morning finds you and your good housekeeper well. My! Just to enter this room reminds me of my first visit to your good household. I can remember as if it was but yesterday those crumpets. Oh, they were so good." He almost dribbled out this last compliment.

"I am sorry, Mrs Jones doesn't have any this morning, but we can have some tea."

With this, he called to Mrs Jones, and she called back that tea would be served in just a moment or two. She was as good as her word, and, as the Captain settled into a proffered chair, a tray was carried into the room. His eyes lighted on the plate that balanced precariously on the edge of the table as she left the room. He stood and made a grab for it, as if rescuing an expensive vase from falling to the floor. He missed his hold, and the plate and its contents scattered across the floor. Embarrassed, he got to his knees and met the rector coming round the other side of the desk on his knees. He managed to retrieve half a scone.

The rector looked up, and, as their eyes met, he laughed and said merrily, "Captain Williams, it is a good place to be, on our knees together, but I fear we are here on mundane matters."

The Captain blushed, stood to his full, if short, height, and apologised for the mess. He did manage to lick the butter from his fingers, and he stuffed half a scone into his cheeks as he sat down again. Mrs Jones came in and brushed up the crumbs, and the rector opened up a conversation.

"My dear Captain," said the rector, putting the man at his ease again, "I am happy to see you at any time, but do you have some special business with me today? I am wondering just when the day will come when you will win the hand and heart of one of your lady friends in the village. I would count it a great pleasure to conduct your wedding, you know. Just to see you happily settled and catered for would reassure us that you were a part of the life of the community and here to stay."

"My dear rector, you make me blush, officer though I am. There are many kind ladies who, from time to time, proffer a little repast and brighten the life of an old soldier, but none as yet has hazarded her life to the hands of the King's man."

"Beautifully said, sir – but one day, one day!"

"Quite so, quite so!" concluded the Captain. "But let me

ask you a question, good rector."

"Yes, you may ask as you please, for if it's not marriage you have come about, I am at a loss to know your business."

"My question is simple, sir. Some time ago you paid a visit to France. Oh, you need not worry how I got to hear; my good friend at the Terrapin told me he saw you return. But I am intrigued, good sir, as to your business in such a land at this time. I hear there are many things happening which speak of anarchy and even treachery in military circles."

"You are well informed, Captain. What I saw in Paris was not pleasant, and I have little desire to visit that land again, but you intrigue me as to why you interest yourself."

"Oh, that is easily explained, sir. I have followed the exploits of the London gentleman who from time to time, we hear, rescued some from the guillotine. I have wondered what will happen now that he has been exposed."

"That will be interesting to watch, Captain – very interesting. But now, seeing we both have such an interest in events on the other side of the Channel, might I ask if you would seriously like to make the crossing and see for yourself what is happening there?"

The Captain was taken aback. He stuttered and said he had not thought of taking such a trip, but he told the rector he might consider it if enough time were given for him to prepare.

The rector explained that the trip would be for but a brief day or so, and they could be sure he would not be long away from his duties in the parish. Two weeks to the day was the agreed date of departure, and when the Captain left the rectory he was hardly able to contain his elation that he was actually being taken into the rector's confidence.

He carefully wrote a note to Latreque and sent it with Ben Pearson, Lower Penzle's ageing carter, whose even older horse seemed some days as if he might never quite make the two-way journey, brief as it was, from the village to Crendon Bywater.

The day of the voyage was bright and windy. The journey across to France was a pleasant one, and the heavy case of books the rector carried was taken off by two seamen and placed in a carriage awaiting hire at the quayside as they landed.

The rector and the Captain laughed together as they recalled with Captain Storeton the events of the rector's smuggling days. It was not until they were getting into the carriage to move off to Paris that the rector saw what confirmed his thoughts about this strange interest the Captain had expressed in France. There, in another carriage, sat Monsieur Latreque, shading his face with his hand, but unmistakable to the rector's sharp eye. So this was the game! Our friendly officer was in the employ of Latreque, and their every move was being watched. Well, if that was the case, the rector had his plans laid too.

The two men agreed to visit the parts of Paris they were interested in together, and then the rector had some books he wished to sell in second-hand bookshops. He would be some hours going from shop to shop. The Captain could watch for himself the events of the day at the place of execution and see Madame Guillotine do her foul work. As they parted, they agreed to make their own way back to the ship by nightfall and either sleep on board at Captain Storeton's invitation or board first thing in the morning, when the *Sea Winkle* would catch the tide.

When the morning came, a stiff bundle of humanity eased itself out of the wooden bunk and eyed the weather. It was thick with mist and little wind. They might miss the tide, but at least that meant the rector would have time to make the sailing, for somehow he had failed to gain the ship by nightfall. In fact, he did not show up at all. When Captain Storeton gave orders to cast off to meet the afternoon tide, Willoughby Williams scanned the dockside in vain for his man. The rector had missed the boat.

During the voyage, Captain Williams made several attempts

to gain the attention of an elderly man and his very plump wife. The man was obviously stone deaf, and his wife was a shy, giggling lady a good deal younger than her husband. The man had a heavy beard with mutton-chop whiskers that stood out from his cheeks and swept up to his hat. The lady wore a heavy cloak, and they sat for the whole journey in the shelter of the deckhouse on their one large travel trunk. It was not until they were alighting at Crendon Bywater that the officer noted that the case was identical to that which the rector had used for his many books.

"I must tell the rector of this coincidence when I see him next. I wonder how he will make the journey?"

The journey from France was slow and tedious for all on board the *Sea Winkle*. The mist which held them in port in the morning barely lifted, and the lack of wind made Captain Storeton tack many times before finally sailing into Crendon Bywater that evening.

Imagine Captain Williams' surprise when, after a hearty meal at the Terrapin Inn, he was startled by the voice of the rector, asking for him by name.

"How in the world did you get across the Channel?"

"Oh, you need not worry. I did not engage an angel to wing me across. I was, in fact, on the same boat as you, but I had a little experience which I shall tell you all about on the way home. I have Ben Pearson outside with his cart. If you don't mind my company, we'll make it home before the day is completely gone."

As the two men sat huddled against each other, the rector asked Captain Williams if he had seen an elderly gentleman with a case like the rector's. Willoughby Williams excitedly said he had, and that he had intended to speak of the coincidence.

"That, my dear sir, was no coincidence. That was my case, and I had a terrible job to persuade the gentleman sitting on it to allow me to open it and prove that it was mine and not his. That is the reason why I could not sit with you. I was intent on not leaving them a moment. I had thoughts that this was connected with some criminal game they were playing, but I assure you they were quite harmless and my fears were dispelled. As you can see for yourself, I have my case safe and sound. But, I'm sorry to say, it is still heavy with books I did not sell."

If Captain Williams had asked to see the books, he might have asked the rector why along with his theological volumes there was a set of mutton-chop whiskers, a top hat and some spare clothing; but he didn't ask another question, and the two men parted. Captain Williams made his weary way to the attic room and bed, and the rector enjoyed telling Mrs Jones his story all over again.

"And who was your 'wife', rector?"

"Oh, that I must not tell, my dear Mrs Jones – that I must not tell. But, to do the lady justice, when she boarded the Plymouth coach she had lost a good few pounds of weight and you would not have recognised her for the same lady at all."

CHAPTER EIGHT

The Shipwreck

Storms had been battering the south-west coast of England for days, and the *Sea Winkle* had missed sailing its normal route on each tide. Captain Storeton eyed the weather as the evening darkened, and he was thankful not to have taken advantage of a lull in the storm during the day to slip his moorings and make for the open sea.

"I pity anyone out in the Channel tonight. The storm is nowhere near blowing itself out."

The landlord of the Terrapin Inn agreed and went about his business serving his guests. If the weather was bad for sailing, it was good for business. The several passengers awaiting the *Sea Winkle*'s voyage to France were seated around the blazing fire or at the tables of the inn, glad too that they were not on the high seas that night.

Captain Storeton threw his cloak around his broad shoulders and went out into the wind and the rain. At the stables of the inn he told the stable boy to saddle a horse, and in a few minutes he galloped out of the yard and made for the high road to Lower Penzle.

The rain was intermittent, and the Captain found the ride across the moor exhilarating. His life was spent in the wind and the fresh sea air. Shore life often suffocated him, but he enjoyed this ride. As he came to the old mill at the top of the hill leading down to Lower Penzle, he stopped his mount and surveyed the dark stretch of sea below the cliffs. What little light there was came from a shy moon that showed itself occasionally, flitting in and out of the clouds. There across the bay his sharp eyes caught sight of a ship riding out the storm. It was a sizeable barque, certainly bigger than his own *Sea Winkle*, but no ship could ride easily such waves as were lifting and twisting and rolling this lady of the sea. She rolled so far in the wind that the Captain whistled as he waited for her to come upright again. She was in trouble, that was for sure. Either her cargo was shifting or she had sprung a leak. She lay for a long while on her side, and then sluggishly righted herself, only to be laid low again as the wind caught her and took her down into a great trough of water. When he next saw her, she was fully on her side, her masts lying along the water.

He gasped, hoping that she might even yet recover herself, but she lay wallowing in spray and a wave broke clean over her side and poured water across her decks. For some minutes he lost sight of her and thought she had turned right over; but then, to his amazement, when the moon came out again she had recovered a little and was turning in towards the shore.

Captain Storeton waited no longer. The ship was a mile from shore in deep water. If her master was skilled in handling his ship, she might reach the shore. If he knew Lower Penzle Harbour, he might even make that small haven. But with such a sea running he would need a light to guide him in. The Captain rode down into the village and to the harbour wall.

He was not the only one aware of the ship's plight. Several men were there, and the light keeper was busy lighting the lantern atop the small stone tower at the end of the harbour wall.

As if watching for such a light, the master of the wallowing ship flashed a lantern in the direction of the harbour. There was distress in every flash. The wind was blowing right up from the Atlantic and driving the ship inshore at a fast rate. Ahead of it were the rocks and coves for which this shore is notorious.

Wreckers had often lured ships on to the rocks to plunder their cargoes, but this night every man in the village rode out on a mission of mercy to await the impact of the great wooden hulk that drifted nearer by the moment to its doom.

On board the Captain eyed the coastline. There was a cove ahead of him, and he hoisted a sail and steered for it. But the sea and wind were no friends to the mariners on the ship, who were pitting their wits against these elemental forces of nature. The tide caught the great ship and moved its sluggish bulk broadside to the shore.

When it hit the first time, the sound of crushing timbers could be heard by those above them on the cliff top. Lanterns were swung as men clambered down to whatever ledge they could find, but the ship was lifted and crushed again and again on the razor-sharp rocks.

Even such a large vessel could take only so much pounding, and when morning dawned it was clear to the onlookers that she could not last long before breaking her back or capsizing as the sea hammered her port side. Several times during the night cries had been heard from the ship as the crew tried to make contact with their would-be rescuers, but the wind and the crashing waves left no opportunity for their words to be heard. Then, as the morning brightened and the tide began to leave the lower rocks more accessible, Captain Storeton, the rector and other able-bodied men climbed down and waited. If the ship broke up, those on board would have to take their chances in the water, and it was hoped that when the time came the great hulk would be close enough to the shore to give the swimmers a fighting chance.

Heavy with water, the ship gradually lay over on its shoreward side and made a pool of comparatively calm water between itself and the shore. One of the young village men entered the water and tried to swim to the ship with a rope. Several times he was lifted off his feet and thrown dangerously near to the rocks, but at last he got into deep water and swam with some effort out towards the ship. On board he rested, and then he entered the water again and swam back to the rocks. Others waded out in the water to drag him clear, and then they made fast the rope between the ship and the shore. The first man from the ship was a seaman with a baby on his back; the second one helped a young woman hand over hand along the swaying rope. As they came, their bodies were caught by the surging waters and tossed back and forth. The drama heightened when the rector recognised none other than Latreque following hard along the rope after the young woman. With her clothing ripped by the ordeal, the young woman was covered with a cloak and reunited with her baby. Latreque seemed little concerned with the rescue of anyone else as he followed the woman up the cliff face to the high path at the top.

"Monsieur Latreque!" The voice of the rector stopped Latreque in his climb. "You must come to the rectory and dry your clothes."

The rector's invitation was sincere, but it was also an attempt to prevent the Frenchman following too closely the steps of the young woman he was so obviously interested in.

"*Monsieur le Recteur*, you are once again very kind, but I fear business requires my attention. I am already delayed two days by the storm, and, having escaped with our lives, those of us with urgent business must proceed on our way."

"You have a companion, then? I did not see another man from the ship when we left the rocks. It is doubtful that many will be rescued before she breaks up, and none could survive long in that turbulent water. I have great fear for most on board."

"You need have little fear," replied Latreque. "There were but three passengers, and we are all off. The crew will make it if the rope holds."

"Am I to understand that you and the young woman and the baby are related?"

"You are altogether too inquisitive, good sir."

127

With these words, Latreque made to turn and continue his climb up the path.

"The young woman, whoever she is, and her small child must at least get warm, dry clothing, Monsieur. I insist that she come to the rectory to recuperate from her ordeal; otherwise I fear she will catch her death of cold."

"I thank you, good rector, for your concern, but the lady is in my care and we shall lodge the night in the Terrapin at Crendon Bywater."

Latreque was so abrupt that the rector felt a genuine sense of guilt at being so insistent. Yet why, if this young woman were travelling with Latreque, did she not wait for him? Already she had been placed in a cart at the top of the hill and, at her request, she was being driven down into the village.

She was taken into the White Horses and conducted to a bedroom. A warm fire blazed before her as she disrobed, and, with blankets around her, she fed her baby quietly as maids came and went with clothing and more fuel for the fire.

Latreque commandeered a second cart and followed, as he thought, the young woman into Crendon Bywater. Too late he realised that being so near to Lower Penzle the woman and baby were more likely to have gone to that village. The carter turned his horse slowly and retraced his steps. Latreque sneezed heavily, his wet clothes still clinging miserably about his body.

"Can't you get this old horse to even trot?" he asked angrily.

Ben Pearson misheard the question and shouted back that he would not charge for the journey to Crendon Bywater, but would have to ask for something for the change of direction.

Latreque did not answer, but he fell to thinking how he could get his quarry out of Lower Penzle without interference from the rector.

Thinking the rector would already have taken the young woman into his care, Latreque booked a room at the inn and stripped in its privacy and warmth. He wrapped himself in a blanket, and a serving man took his clothes to dry them. Then he heard with disgust the voice of the rector asking if he might see another guest when she was able to entertain a visitor. He then knew full well that his quarry was still in the inn; but if the rector were to talk with her, all was lost.

He rose to his feet, hurried to the door of his room and called along the passage: "Is that you, *Monsieur le Recteur*? If you have a moment, may I talk with you?"

The rector was surprised to hear Latreque's voice. He assumed that he had taken the Crendon Bywater road as he had suggested he would.

"Why, of course, my friend. What can I do for you?"

"Come into my room, Monsieur. I fear this night's ordeal has taken its toll on even my strong constitution." With this, he sneezed into his blanket.

"My good sir, you should retire to bed and get thoroughly warmed, or you will lose your health altogether."

"I have been thinking again of your kind offer, good sir. As I find myself without bags or money, staying here is out of the question. I am not known to the good innkeeper, so I cannot impose myself on his generosity. Maybe if I could accept your own good offer, I and my companions could stay with you overnight and then return to Crendon Bywater together when we are able."

"Of course you may, and it will be my good pleasure – though you need not have worried yourself about the good innkeeper. Jeremiah is as generous a man as you will find anywhere. I will tell him of your intentions, and we shall arrange for you all to be brought up to the rectory in the morning after you have had a good night's rest."

"Rector, you are a gentleman!"

"I trust I am, sir. Now I will leave you to have a meal. Good day to you."

The rector bowed and left the room. He made his way down the stairs, gave his word to Jeremiah Solent, and left to walk up the hill to the rectory.

CHAPTER NINE

The Disappearing Lady

As the clock struck eight in the parlour of the White Horses, Mrs Jones, the rector's housekeeper, walked through the door and found herself face-to-face with Monsieur Latreque.

"Ah, there you are, sir. I trust you had a good night's rest and feel no harm from your terrible ordeal. I hear the captain of your ship was lost this morning when she broke her back. Poor man! They say he was swimming ashore when the mast hit him, and he was not seen again. It's a mercy every one of you was not lost."

Mrs Jones would have gone on to preach a good sermon on the mercy of God had her French listener let her. But he cut her short and asked if there was word from the rector for him.

"Why, bless you, sir! That's the very reason I am here. He would like you and the lady to be with us sometime this morning, if you and the lady feel like coming up the hill. Oh, the rector is asking Mr Peirpoint to bring you. He's the undertaker, you know."

"Madame, your rector is most kind. I have escaped death by just a little and he sends the undertaker to carry me."

Mrs Jones saw the funny side, and they both laughed heartily.

"Please tell the good rector I will be ready when Mr Purspoint comes."

"Mr Peirpoint is the name, sir. Yes, I'll tell the rector you will be with us."

As Mrs Jones went through the parlour to see her sister, the innkeeper's wife, she caught sight of the young lady and her baby. It was too much for her curiosity to pass her by, and she sailed into a conversation by giving thanks for her safe rescue from the ship. Mrs Jones realised the lady did not understand English; but when she spoke to the baby, the bright-eyed little child smiled and won Mrs Jones in a moment.

"Wonderful, it is, to be sure!" she said half to herself. "The little mite can't speak, but she knows I'll love her up there at the rectory."

Mrs Jones hurried out through the door into the innkeeper's living quarters, and Latreque and the lady were left alone. He spoke quickly in French, and even a casual observer would have noted the strain between them.

An hour later, the rescued French trio were in the rector's study.

"*Monsieur le Recteur*, I must introduce my wife's sister and her child. I am afraid she does not speak a word of English, and she is very overwrought after her experience. She was running away from her husband when I discovered her aboard the ship bound for England. I shall be taking her back to her family as soon as the weather permits a sailing from Crendon Bywater."

"I am pleased to meet you, madam," said the rector, not using French, as he could so easily have done.

Maybe this young lady was related to Latreque, and maybe not, but the rector made as though he accepted the explanation. He entered into the idea by asking if there had been trouble in the marriage.

"My dear rector, many families are divided in France today by the political and social upheaval. This young lady does not appreciate the great future that France is set for as we purge ourselves of the aristocratic sickness."

"Quite so, Monsieur! We shall do all we can to make you both comfortable, and I will send a message to ask Captain

Storeton to inform us of his next sailing."

"You are too, too kind, sir. I marvel at your willingness to help us, when I know you have great reserves about our country's revolutionary movement."

"I cannot deny that everything about the revolution leaves me thankful that England has a good king on the throne and we still have our faith in God."

"Ah, good sir, I do not want to enter into a dispute with you – you have been so kind to us – but I think the faith of the people of France did them little good when they were starving and the aristocracy was feasting."

The conversation died and the rector left the room to attend to his morning's work. He left the door open, however, and took the liberty to listen as Latreque spoke harshly to the woman. It soon became plain to the rector that he had been told anything but the truth. This young woman was more than a family runaway. He heard Latreque warn her that she would not reach France alive if she so much as hinted who she was. Latreque had obviously gone to great trouble to follow her and did not mean to lose her now.

The day passed with meals and rest, and at bedtime they all retired carrying their lamps up the stairs to separate rooms.

During the night Mrs Jones was disturbed at her end of the house by the sound of the baby crying, and she quickly ran to the young woman's bedroom to see if she needed anything. It was obvious that the child was too upset to return to sleep, and Mrs Jones signalled to the lady to follow her downstairs into her back kitchen. There Mrs Jones stoked up the smouldering embers of the fire and threw on more wood to make a cheerful blaze. The lady was obviously pleased to have company and she appreciated Mrs Jones' kindness. She suckled her child and sang softly to it. She tried to speak to Mrs Jones. She thanked her in French, and Mrs Jones understood her meaning though she knew none of the words.

Then the young lady asked a question: "*Monsieur le Recteur et Monsieur Latreque sont amis, nest-ce pas?*"

"Oh dear! I don't quite know what you mean, my dear."

The young woman repeated her words and acted out a little mime of two people embracing.

Mrs Jones thought she understood. She shook her head and said that the rector and her guardian were not exactly friends.

The woman had heard the word *friend* before, and she continued: "*Monsieur Latreque est non friend,*" and she pointed to herself. "*Je parle le recteur, oui, mon amie.*" She pointed to herself, and up to the ceiling for the rector.

Mrs Jones thought she understood.

"You would like to speak with the rector in the morning?"

The young woman shook her head when she recognised the word *morning*. She pointed to the little clock on the mantelshelf, walked up to it and pointed to the present time.

"You mean you would like to speak to the rector now?"

The young woman guessed that Mrs Jones had understood, and she nodded her head very violently, grasping Mrs Jones' arm and bending her knee in a kind of curtsy.

Mrs Jones left the room, feeling that the matter must be urgent and that she should at least wake the rector and tell him of what she thought was a request to speak with him.

When he at last entered the room, he spoke in fluent French, and the young woman stood and embraced him with her free arm, holding the baby in the other. He explained that he understood that she was in trouble, and he said he would gladly help if he could. He asked if Latreque had been telling the truth when she said she was running away from her husband.

She quickly told the rector that the story had no truth in it, and that her husband was, in truth, Jack Dart. She had been fleeing from France, and she had already paid her passage and was on board when the Captain disclosed her presence to Latreque, who had come on board seeking her.

The rector quickly formed a plan in his mind.

He told Mrs Jones to go upstairs and get the woman's clothes and take them into the study.

Unfortunately, as she reached the top of the stairs, Latreque came from his room.

"Is there something wrong with Madame?" he enquired with some anxiety in his voice.

"Oh, it's just the baby – bless her! She is having a little difficulty sleeping. It'll be the terrible happenings she has been through. She'll be all right in a day or two."

Latreque went to the head of the stairs and listened. Hearing no other voice, he ventured down. When he entered the back kitchen, where he had seen the lamp lit, the young woman was alone with her baby. The tall pantry door stood ajar, and the rector's tall figure stood in its shadows, but Latreque saw no one. He quickly restated his threat to the young girl, who winced and slumped back in her chair.

Latreque left, and he met Mrs Jones coming down the stairs with a heavy blanket; but underneath was hidden the clothing of the young woman.

She carried it into the study and said in a rather loud voice, "Come in here, my dear, and I'll make you comfortable by the fire. The rector won't mind you lying on his couch for the night. You will be warmer than in that cold bedroom."

The young woman went into the study, and, when she had dressed, the rector followed her in on tiptoe. He had been listening to make sure Latreque was no longer still about. He whispered to Mrs Jones to make up a fire, but first to get his own clothing from his room under yet another blanket. This she did, and he hurriedly donned them over his night attire. Bidding the young woman take the blanket for her baby, he touched the hidden latch and the bookcase swung forward to reveal the secret passageway to the amazed eyes of the young Frenchwoman.

He then beckoned her to follow him carefully down the winding stair. He carried a lantern in his hand and bade her be most careful of the rugged stone steps.

When they were at the bottom, he explained in French that they would soon be out into the night at the church exit from this tunnel.

As dawn broke, Latreque made his way quietly down the stairs and into the rector's study. Some blankets lay in a heap on the floor by the empty couch, but the young woman and the baby were nowhere to be seen. Quickly he walked to the back kitchen, but there was no sign of anyone. He leapt up the stairs, two at a time, and entered the woman's bedroom. She was gone and so was her clothing. He ran back down the stairs and inspected the front door locks. They were all secure.

Rudely he shouted for the rector, who came sleepily out of his bedroom asking what the matter was.

"She is gone – the woman is gone. She must have fled in the night after sleeping in your study. She must have used a window or a back door. The hall door is still bolted. *Monsieur le Recteur*, you must lend me your horse. I must find her. She cannot have gone far in the night; she will no doubt be in the village."

"You are right," said the rector. "Of course you may borrow my horse. I will follow you on foot to the village."

Latreque dressed himself and helped to saddle the horse. Then he was gone as if on the wind.

CHAPTER TEN

Lost in the Night

As Pierre Latreque galloped to a halt outside the White Horses, there was little activity to be seen. He tethered the rector's horse and tried the front door. It was unlocked, and he entered. A maid was busy cleaning, and she curtsied to him.

"The master isn't about yet, sir. Can I get you something?"

"You can tell me something, young woman! Did the young woman and her baby come here early this morning?"

"Why, yes, sir. I heard the master open up in the early hours and I heard a baby crying. I expect they are sleeping yet, sir."

"Then I will wait for them. Thank you for your information."

Latreque settled in the fireless chimney corner and awaited the stirring of the inn and its inhabitants.

He mused on the fact that the woman had made her way here in the night and awakened everyone. Would she not guess that he would follow and find her at daybreak? As he mused, the door opened and the rector came in, red-faced after his brisk morning walk. The cold light of the morning shone in through the cracks in the shutters, and the creaking boards of the floors above told of guests and staff awakening.

Within the half-hour both the rector and Latreque were drinking hot drinks, and the smell of cooking awakened their appetites as they discussed the possible reasons for the young woman leaving the rectory in the middle of the night. The rector was amazed how calm Latreque seemed, having lost his captive. Yet he knew more than Latreque, and he listened, not a little amused, as Latreque told him of his concern for the distressed woman. How he would have liked to tear down that facade and tell Latreque the whole truth! But time would tell the Frenchman all he needed to know, and by then his quarry would be lost.

As the two men were enjoying a hearty breakfast of eggs and large slices of ham cooked to a turn by the newly lit fire, Willoughby Winton Williams came in, puffing and blowing as if he had been for a morning swim.

"Ah, my good sir—" he blurted out as he crossed the room to Latreque.

Then he saw the rector. Seeing the two men together mystified him. They looked as if a friendship was between them, yet Williams knew they were working on two sides opposed to each other.

"May I speak to you alone, sir?" he apologetically asked.

"You may, good sir, but perhaps you would be good enough to wait till I have completed my breakfast and my conversation with the good rector here."

The man was a little put out by this rebuff, but he contented himself with the thought that he had not missed breakfast and he sat down in the rear parlour to enjoy a large helping of porridge and eggs and ham.

He was still tucking in to as much fresh bread as he could when the innkeeper appeared and greeted him with a heavy pat on the back. Williams nearly choked on his mouthful of breakfast. He coughed and spluttered, and then grunted his "Good morning" to his genial host. The landlord went through to greet his new guests.

"Good morning, gentlemen. It is an honour to have you both at my table so early. And what brings you to the village at such an hour?"

"Oh, I have come down to meet Madame and the baby.

They returned to your fine inn last night, I understand."

"Indeed they did," said the innkeeper. He then continued, half to himself: "It was a fine time for a young woman and child to be making the journey to the high road to catch the Plymouth coach. I am surprised they caught it; they must have followed it some way before getting it to stop. I know that coachman, and he will not stop for everyone between towns. He's too aware of the tricks of the highwaymen in these parts. We've had our share of very unpleasant incidents, as the rector will tell you."

"Yes, indeed we have."

Monsieur Latreque rose from his seat, his face turning red as he did so.

"Are you telling me that the lady is not upstairs in bed, landlord?"

"Indeed she isn't, sir. I did just as you asked me to in the note the lady handed me."

"And what note might that be, sir? Show it to me, for I sent no note and no lady. She came here in the middle of the night, and I was under the impression, from what your maid said, that she was still here."

"Then, I'm afraid, sir, that the maid does not know what happened. Indeed, she could not have known, for I only disturbed Captain Williams to take the good lady to the Plymouth coach as you asked."

"As I asked!" Latreque almost shouted. "Bring Monsieur Williams to me. I need to know what all this is about."

Willoughby Winton Williams entered the room, his mouth again full of breakfast.

"Sir, will you tell me where you have been and what exactly you have been doing this morning?"

Captain Williams cleared his throat and mopped his chin.

"Well, Monsieur Latreque, I was awakened at a very early hour by the landlord, and I was asked to dress and take the lady to the Plymouth coach by horse. I am, sir, a soldier, and I am unaccustomed to riding with a lady in the saddle; but, seeing the request was from your good self, I dressed and we rode at as great a speed as we could, though it was uphill and two of us and the child were in the saddle. We had some difficulty in getting the coach to stop, but I am accustomed to command and he thought I was an officer of the law. He stopped and the lady and child were safely put aboard. They will catch the London coach as you wished, I have no fear, for the Plymouth coach was in good time. I must say that it is a long journey for a young woman and baby to take alone, but I did as you requested."

With this, Williams gave a little bow and waited for some commendation.

He was disappointed. Latreque was in a rage. He didn't understand and he was annoyed. He had been tricked, but by whom? His captive had got away and there was not a hope of catching the coach, which was many miles away by now. Even with its brief stop in Crendon Bywater, it was three hours ahead of him. Anyway, what excuse could he give to remove a woman and child from a coach on to which she had been put? He asked to see the note, which the landlord gladly brought. He read it, studying the handwriting. It was clearly not his own hand, but whose it was he could not think. Was it the young woman who had written it? No, she did not know English. It was an educated hand, and signed simply 'L'. He gasped and sat down.

The innkeeper broke in, as he looked at Latreque's obvious mystification:

"Are you saying that you did not write that note and you did not want the young lady to get that coach? Monsieur, I did what I thought you wanted. How was I to know this note was not from you. I do hope you don't think I acted too hastily."

Then Williams, coughing and not a little confused by the whole escapade, said, "I too only did my duty, sir, in helping the lady; and I thought I was helping you."

The Captain sank into a chair as he realised that he had helped Latreque's enemies instead of Latreque. They had all been tricked, but by whom? That was the question they were all now asking. Only the rector sat quietly finishing his breakfast, looking into the leaping flames of the fire. Latreque eyed him, but the rector did not look up. Instead, he thanked the landlord for the fine breakfast and asked Latreque to spend the day with him.

"Indeed I will not, sir. I will make my way to Crendon Bywater and get the first ship back to France."

CHAPTER ELEVEN

A Most Unusual Service

The rector returned to his house on the hill, and Mrs Jones was all ears as he told his tale of the young woman's ride with Captain Williams.

"Oh, I suppose Mr Latreque was very angry to think his own man had been the means of her escape, sir," she said, busying herself tidying the study after the night's events.

"You may be sure of one thing, Mrs Jones: Monsieur Latreque will put two and two together, and he will be all the more sure that we are not helping his cause. I have a feeling that our task of helping those poor French people will be harder from now on." The rector sat down at his desk and noticed a note in front of him. "Did someone come while I was down at the inn, Mrs Jones?"

"Why, no, sir! No one has been here at this hour."

The rector read the note and realised that it must have come from either Latreque or the lady, before she left, for the English was very poor and there was no signature. As the rector read and reread the simple message, Mrs Jones left the room. There was a slight creak of a door on its hinges, the rector turned, and there at the open bookcase stood Jack Dart.

"Jack!" the rector gasped.

"*Mon ami*," Jack replied, rushing to the rector and greeting him with a kiss on each cheek.

They embraced each other, but Jack refused to release his friend, and the rector could feel him sobbing as if his heart was breaking.

"What ails you, my friend? Sit yourself down."

"*Oh, mon ami, mon ami*, my wife and child set sail some days ago and I fear the worst for the ship they travelled in. I saw no masts of it as I sailed past Crendon Bywater this morning. Have you heard of a shipwreck in these parts? I trusted the Captain, and with a large ship he should have made it, but I have no assurance that they even reached these shores. I have withstood so much these last weeks. Rachel's life and my child's life were in danger. I could hold out no longer, but now I fear all may have been lost."

"Jack, do you have faith in God?"

"Monsieur, you have never asked that of me before!"

"No, Jack, but you need just now to realise that you do not work alone."

"I am not understanding you, *mon ami*."

"Well, Jack, I see God at work every day, and I have just seen God at work in a wonderful way."

"Monsieur, what are you trying to tell me?"

"Just this, my dear friend, Jack: your wife and child are safe and well, on their way to London."

"*Grace à Dieu*! But tell me, please tell me: how do you know? I come and find no sign of a ship, yet you tell me you know she is safe and on her way to London."

"Jack, there is a ship. It lies in pieces at the foot of Lynden Tor. Two nights ago our good friend Captain Storeton raised the alarm when he saw her in great trouble nearing the rocks. Every man from the village was down on the shore, and we did all we could, but in that storm no ship could survive. She hit the rocks and turned over, and, as you rightly say, there is no ship to be seen now. Her crew – all but the Captain – were taken off, and, Jack, three passengers."

"Three? But my wife and child were alone when she set sail. Who was the third?"

"Who might you expect, Jack? Our friend – if I dare call him that – Pierre Latreque."

"*Oh, mon Dieu!*"

"Yes, friend Jack, God may well be the only reason why you still have a wife and child. I thanked Him that night, and you give me all the more reason to thank Him this morning that we got her safely out of the hands of that fiend of a revolutionary. When I think of the tale he told of her being his sister-in-law! Later, oh, Jack, I found out who she really was. She did not breathe a word to me till I conversed with her in French when we were out of Latreque's hearing."

"But how, *mon ami*, did you get her away from the wretched animal?"

The rector told his story, and, at the mention of the tunnel, Jack gave a little start.

"Oh, Monsieur, I almost forgot. I came not alone. Down in your tunnel I have seven friends who sailed with me. I did not know what I might find here, so I told them to await my call. They are below in your tunnel."

"Then be so good as to tell them they are more than welcome, Jack. I will tell Mrs Jones we have company."

Mrs Jones remonstrated with the rector, half in fun, that she had nothing prepared for such a crowd.

"And where shall we sleep such a crowd tonight?" she asked, as practical as ever.

"Oh, we'll find room somehow. I do not know if they are men or women till they appear, good woman. Off with you now! And get us all some food, for I breakfasted early, as you know."

She had hardly entered her kitchen when there was a knock at the front door. The rector went, fearful that the caller, whoever he was, might be confronted by a crowd of Frenchmen appearing out of a bookcase. His face drained of colour when he opened the door on none other than Pierre Latreque himself.

"Well, speak of angels and they flap their wings!" the rector joked. "We have just been speaking of you. I thought by now you would be on board the *Sea Winkle*. Surely Captain Storeton has a sailing this fine morning."

"Yes, he has, but I chose not to sail with him. Seeing my sister-in-law has made her way to London, I am going to have to send some letters to warn friends in that city that she will be arriving. I wish I could spare time to go myself."

As Latreque talked on of his fake concern for his fake relative, voices came from the study. The rector spoke louder, and, with a crushing fear that everything would be discovered by Latreque, he asked him by name to step into the sitting room with him. As he did so, he called to Mrs Jones as if she had suddenly become deaf: "Mrs Jones, Monsieur Latreque is here. Make him some strong coffee and I will join him in the sitting room."

Silence reigned within the study as Jack Dart froze at the name *Latreque*. He pushed his friends back down the winding stair and drew the bookcase closed behind him.

'That was a narrow escape, if ever there was one,' he thought.

Silently they listened. Mrs Jones came in with the coffee and the rector followed her back into the room and apologised to Latreque for leaving him.

"The gardener wanted to see me. I thought I heard someone calling me. Come in, John, and meet my French friend. You will remember he was one of those rescued from the ship. Monsieur Latreque, John Prendegast, son of one of my parish councillors, Farmer Edgar Prendegast."

The boy entered and held tight to his cap as he met the imposing figure from France. He left as quickly as he had come, but the rector felt he had saved the day. He hoped that Jack had gone back into the tunnel and would await an all-clear from him.

Pierre Latreque thanked the rector for his coffee and left to take up his abode in the White Horses again. As he would be staying for a further day or so, that complicated matters for Jack and the rector. Tomorrow was Sunday and the rectory would be empty. If these refugees were to be housed and fed, precautions would be needed. Latreque seemed always to turn up at the wrong time – or did he know more than he suggested? Had he seen the French boat? If he hadn't yet, he would do as soon as he went near the harbour.

The rector opened the bookcase door and called to Jack. He was sitting on the top step, but the rector hadn't seen him.

"Jack, you rascal! So there you are! That was the nearest escape we've had yet. We must be doubly careful in future. No one except Mrs Jones and the councillors know of the tunnel; swear your people to secrecy, or all will be lost."

"*Mon ami*, I have already sworn my people to silence, lest their French tongues should be heard anywhere. But how do we get them out of here if Latreque is about? He is like a ferret: he seems to be able to sniff out anything."

"Oh, don't worry – I have it all worked out."

And so he had!

Sunday dawned bright and the sharp wind off the sea brought fresh air into the tunnel as the door opened at the church end. Out climbed seven young men in the robes of Anglican choirboys, complete with ruffles and music sheets. They processed into the morning service and took their places in the choir stalls at the side of the usual choir. Room was made for them, and glances were cast from all over the church at these extra members of the choir. They stood when the choir stood and opened and closed their mouths as the choir sang.

The smallest of St Matthew's choir members whispered to his neighbour, "Why are they not making any noise when they open their mouths?"

Old Joseph Trenbeath whispered back that maybe they were shy, having come as visitors to the church.

That settled the boy, but there was another inquisitive onlooker who might have been much more interested had he been near enough to hear a strong French voice reciting the Lord's Prayer: "*Notre Père, qui êtes aux cieux . . .*"

But the rector quelled all doubts as to who they were and where they had come from when he welcomed them as members of a visiting choir. At that, all questions ceased, and he added that they had to leave early to meet their choirmaster coming from Crendon Bywater.

They left during the hymn before the sermon, missing a good exhortation from the rector, and the inquisitive gaze of Monsieur Latreque followed them.

The sermon was on St Paul's shipwreck, and most of the congregation agreed it was one of John Trevethin's best sermons.

"Very appropriate, sir, very appropriate," said Captain Williams as he left the service a little ahead of Latreque.

Outside the church, during the preaching of that sermon, the choirboys folded their surplices neatly and placed them under the seat of old Ben Pearson's cart. Their choirmaster, otherwise known as Jack Dart, sat at the old carter's side and kept him talking as the 'choir' sang in perfect French some songs which were rather different from hymns of the church. But, with Ben's deafness and the large sum he was being paid for this Sunday trip, he neither noted nor would have cared what language they were singing in. He had agreed to get them all safely to Upton Wendover, where they were to stay overnight to catch the coach to Plymouth. Ben did ask why he couldn't take them to Crendon instead, but they said they were to sing in Upton – and there was no doubt they did sing in Upton as they praised the Rector of Lower Penzle for his hospitality and their escape.

All seven caught the Plymouth coach the next day. It was so crowded that the driver positively refused to pick up Monsieur Latreque as he waited on the high road to Crendon Bywater. Had he looked a little closer, he might have seen amongst the crowd of passengers a certain Jack Dart, but there were some things that even Pierre Latreque missed, ferret though he might be.

CHAPTER TWELVE

The Miller's Story

The miller turned to see who had entered his milling room. He had heard of the rector's new escapades as the two men met often in friendship – this powerfully built Methodist miller and the tall, adventurous Anglican rector. Now standing in the sunlit doorway was a man Henry Gritton, the miller, had heard the rector describe often. Pierre Latreque stooped a little as he entered the low-ceilinged milling room, with its fast-spinning mills. The fresh breeze blowing up from the sea made easy work for Henry as he controlled the flow of grain between the grindstones.

Windmills do not have the great noise of steam-driven machinery, and, apart from the danger of gears, trapdoors, and chutes, one can relax in the dusty atmosphere. It was this that Pierre needed just now. He was disarmed by the easy, gangling walk of the miller as he came over to greet him. The tension and annoyance of missing the coach fell away from him.

"You're welcome to these parts," said the miller affably. "I think I've heard tell of you – Pierre Latreque, isn't it?"

"That is correct, Monsieur, but how is it that you know me?"

"Oh, I be listening to the rector, and 'e keeps me informed of new people hereabouts."

"I gather you must be a loyal member of his parish, Monsieur?"

"Oh, he wouldn't call me that, sir. I am a Methodist, and I'm afraid the rector never sees me in his congregation; but he must be the most open-minded Anglican in these parts, for he shares a great deal with me and I feel his sympathies are very much with John Wesley himself, if the truth were out."

Latreque was disappointed. He thought he might have an ally right here, and a man who, with Williams, might help him to stem the flow of French aristocrats who seemed to be ever getting help to escape the revolutionary regime on mainland France.

"How come you are walking out this morning, sir? I understood that you were anxious to sail back to your country after you escaped from the wreck. God was good to you, sir, that He was. I never saw a more certain end to a ship and its crew than that, but here you are to tell the tale. I trust you be thankin' God for your deliverance, good sir!"

This sermon was about as much as Latreque could stand. He had missed his coach to Crendon Bywater, and now he had to listen to this giant fool of a miller prattle on about God saving him from a shipwreck. He did not want to feel like Paul on some Mediterranean Isle, greeted by the populace as a saint. He felt he needed a little more help from the Devil to get level with this wily rector and his gang.

The miller invited Latreque to drink with him, but Latreque could not imagine anything worth drinking from a Methodist household. He had heard of their rigorous discipline. He excused himself and was just leaving when the miller asked what time the French ship was sailing from the harbour.

Pierre Latreque spun around.

"Did you say French ship? In Lower Penzle Harbour?"

"Why yes! I thought it had come to collect you."

"*Oui, oui, Monsieur*. I am delighted you mention the fact. I was not aware that it had come. I thank you – I thank you, good miller. I must hurry or they will not know I am still here."

He wrapped his cloak around him and strode out of the mill.

The miller watched him go, and he felt in his bones that this man was evil. The rector was right: this man represented everything that was godless and inhuman about the new order over the Channel.

Pierre Latreque reached the harbour and saw the ship, a French fishing vessel, tied up at the quayside. He made his way as casually as he could to its side. There was no one aboard but a dog. Latreque looked about him. Nothing stirred on the quay. He climbed down the ladder, roped to the stone wall, and stepped on board. The dog growled. Latreque eyed the scruffy guard of the little vessel with its fish-smelling baskets and nets.

'Taisez-vous!' Latreque said as he passed within inches of the snapping jaws. The dog snarled and retreated to its resting place on top of a folded net with its ears back and its tail tucked between its legs. It was used to rough treatment, and it expected a kick to reinforce the command to be quiet.

The Frenchman looked about him for a place to hide, but he was too slow – one of the crew had seen him clamber aboard and came to investigate. Latreque did not hesitate long enough for the man to ask his identity. He barked out a request and identified himself all in one brief sentence.

"When are you sailing back to France? I am Pierre Latreque of the People's Court."

The man whistled long and low.

"So, Monsieur, we are honoured."

The sarcasm in his voice was not missed by Latreque.

"I need to be in France by nightfall. Will you sail this forenoon?"

"Oui, Monsieur, nous mettons à la voile à la marée haute."

And sail on the high tide they did. In silence Latreque sat in the stern of the little ship as she headed out into the keen breeze which had freshened and changed direction to speed the little craft across the miles that separated England from the French Revolution.

Latreque listened as the men worked at their nets, and his unasked question was answered. Why had they come to Lower Penzle at all? Obviously they had not caught any fish, and they were not planning to set their nets on their return trip. Someone had hired them to sail across from France, and, even though he could only catch a word here and there in the banter which fisherman spend their days in, he gathered that their passengers had been good singers.

"Singers?" Pierre said to himself. "Could it be that the rector's visiting choir had actually come from France? Had he again been foiled by this wily Anglican priest?"

CHAPTER THIRTEEN

Latreque's Last Friend Is Lost

Jack Dart stepped off the *Sea Winkle* as she tied up in the French port. The ship had been delayed by bad weather many days and trading merchants were anxiously awaiting all that she had brought. Jack did not slacken his pace as officers hurried to inspect cargo or welcome passengers. Few travellers came to France unless on urgent business. Educational trips to the great European seats of learning were few during these troubled days, and such passengers as came were often officials returning from ambassadorial duties, having tried to persuade their English counterparts that things were settling down in France. One officer saw Dart and, recognising him, made a note to report his presence, but Dart himself made his way through a maze of narrow streets to his transport to Paris. Another group of young Frenchmen had been transported to safety and an English education. Their parents, many of whom would never meet up with them again, could be informed that their family names would live on in freedom. Jack felt a sense of satisfaction.

The note on Pierre Latreque's desk gave him no satisfaction at all. It told him that he had not only missed the Crendon Bywater coach and, in turn, the *Sea Winkle*, but he had missed a chance to arrest Jack Dart himself. Whatever else he did today, he resolved to double the watch on the *Sea Winkle*'s sailings and double his search for this man who had eluded him.

Across the Channel, Willoughby Winton Williams was smarting still from the ridicule he had endured after aiding the escape of Latreque's prize capture. How could he have got himself back into this crazy life of hunting and losing his quarry? Had he not retired from all this when his army days were over? What made it all the worse for his morale was knowing that the rector must be involved. Innocently he had asked the rector why the visiting choirboys had not sung some special choral work to the parishioners of St Matthew's. The rector had passed his question off with some excuse of their having been under great strain. He said they were due in London soon, and they would need all their vocal skills unimpaired. Only after a letter from his French paymaster did the Captain realise all over again how foolish he must appear before all who had known the truth about their identity. He resolved to succeed, and to do so he knew he must develop a closer friendship with the rector.

He called more often at the rectory, and yet the more often he called, the more often he felt that he might become implicated in another plot against his French friends. He also kept as close an eye as he could on the *Sea Winkle*, and it was on one of his journeys with old Ben Grundle to view the arrival of that good ship that he made another discovery of something going on at the rectory.

Ben rounded the corner that led his old horse down the slope to Crendon Bywater Harbour. There, already tied up at the quay, was the *Sea Winkle*. Most of the passengers had already disembarked, and Captain Williams was annoyed at the slow pace of Ben Grundle's cart. He was annoyed to think that he might have missed the opportunity to note any well-dressed men and women, or any strangers that could be travelling in disguise. On this occasion he was too late. He was awakened from his gloomy thoughts by the Rector of Lower Penzle.

"Good morning, Captain Williams!"

"Oh, good morning to you, rector!"

The surprise in his voice was accompanied by a long head-turning look as he counted the four horsemen trailing the rector.

'One, two, three, four! Dear me, dear me – I just wonder who they are?' he asked himself. 'I must make some enquiries.'

This he did, at the Terrapin Inn, at the ship, and of anyone who would talk on the quay, but all he could learn was that they had come on the ship, and the horses had been sent by the rector to await them. They certainly weren't men of the cloth. By their clothing they fitted the pattern of French aristocracy, but Captain Williams was left unsure if they had actually come from France. His French paymaster had assured him that none would escape boldly undisguised, but these well-dressed men could have been dressed by the court tailors themselves.

Ben Grundle returned to Lower Penzle with his cart loaded. He was glad to have a companion up front with him. As they trotted along Captain Williams recalled his first ride with the deaf old carter and tried not to encourage too much conversation, but the countryside resounded to old Ben's rasping voice and the Captain's occasional attempts to make himself heard.

Finally, they reached Lower Penzle High Street, and Williams paid the old carter his two shillings and went into his hostelry for tea. There, to his amazement, were the men he had seen that morning – all four of them without the rector. They were leaving their table, where they had obviously had a mouth-watering feast in the middle of the afternoon.

"Maybe", mused the retired officer of the Crown, "the landlord will put on a special feast this night for his guests and I may even myself be invited."

On enquiring, he groaned inwardly. They were to dine at the rectory! But imagine his ecstasy when, an hour later, he received an invitation to make his way to the rectory and join the party.

He could not believe his good fortune. Now he would be able to satisfy his curiosity and, more importantly (though he would have denied any such suggestion), satisfy his never decreasing appetite.

"Come in, my dear Captain Williams, sir!" called the rector as Williams puffed and panted in the hallway.

Mrs Jones' sister was there to take his coat. She had come from the inn to assist her sister with the large dinner party. The guests around the rector were all speaking fluent French, but they stopped as the new guest entered.

"Allow me to introduce my four French guests," said the rector boldly.

Captain Williams took each hand and then bowed his usual little pompous bow and announced his full name and rank.

The guests each replied in a chorus of *bonjour*s.

The Captain bowed again.

He did not dispel the atmosphere of enjoyment by asking formal questions of identity (or by suggesting that Monsieur Latreque might like to be here!). He was thinking of how he might inform Latreque about this company when the rector broke into the conversation to speak to the Captain.

"My dear Captain, Monsieur Latreque's friends are staying here just for one night before going on to London."

There was silence on the part of the Frenchmen when Latreque's name was mentioned, but Captain Williams rose to the occasion by introducing himself all over again as a personal friend of Monsieur Latreque. This news was accepted, though Captain Williams wondered if they understood. They went on speaking in French, and just now and again the rector would dart a word or two towards him.

During the meal he was in no state to think about conversation. The Captain relaxed in what he considered high company and he enjoyed a great meal. Mrs Jones went down on the Captain's mental list of eligible ladies for marriage –

not by reason of age or beauty, but purely for her culinary ability.

"This is an excellent meal," he said as he submerged himself in the soup.

The party came to an end and the guests left and made their way to the inn for their night's lodging. The Captain would have walked with them, but the rector asked him if he would be so kind as to wait a little till Mrs Jones' sister was ready to be escorted home. He willingly sat back in his chair, and, before a few moments had passed, he sank into a blissful sleep, dreaming of crab and chicken legs all over again.

In the morning Captain Williams was looking through his attic window as four horsemen left the inn yard. Where they were going he did not know, but he was delighted that friends of Monsieur Latreque had met him. He hoped they would tell their friend of his being honoured with a seat at the rector's table.

Latreque, in fact, knew nothing of such a meeting, for the 'friends' were not his friends at all. That had been the rector's sense of humour. They were in truth four key escapees from the Bastille. The Captain hadn't understood a word they said, and the rector's feigned ignorance of French never struck the retired officer as strange.

When at their next meeting the Captain gave details of the men to Latreque, the Frenchman swore an oath to bring the rector to French justice. The Captain was shocked at his outburst, and he even ventured to remind Latreque that the rector was an Englishman and a minister of the church. Latreque retorted that one day, Englishman or not, he, Latreque, would settle this smuggler once and for all. The Captain waited only long enough to be dismissed, and he then went up to his room. What had he gained from the arrogant Frenchman but rebuffs and a great sense of failure? He sat at his little writing table and wrote a formal letter of resignation and then left it addressed to Latreque in the parlour of the inn. He would spy for him no more!

Latreque carried the unopened letter in his pocket till he was way out at sea. As he read it, he laughed sarcastically.

"Does that little eating machine think I care for his services? What has he done but bring ridicule on me and the nation I stand for? Good luck to him. I owe him not a cent. I am glad to be rid of his services. If that is the British Army, we will have no trouble in defeating them on the field when the time comes."

He threw the letter to the wind and the waves.

CHAPTER FOURTEEN

Reconciliation

Sitting at the end of the harbour wall in the fresh morning breeze, Captain Willoughby Winton Williams gazed above him to watch a gull wheel and turn into the wind. It hung there motionless, riding the air currents; only its head turned, one way and then the other, seeking food for its next meal. Then, as the Captain's gaze was drawn down and away from the bird, his eyes lighted on a young couple strolling arm in arm along the harbour wall towards him.

At first he did not recognise them, but as they drew near he saw two people with whom he had had not one conversation since retiring to Lower Penzle. The reason for this absence of contact lay in the events of a year earlier, for they were none other than Mr and Mrs Donald Creedy. Donald was a young stripling of a man; Lizzie, his wife, was a regular dumpling, round and red of complexion and hair. The Captain's use of Lizzie Slocum, as she then was, to capture the smugglers was known throughout the village. The trap had only been set because the Captain had traded on the hurt feelings of young Lizzie, whose courtship with Donald had been interrupted by his smuggling escapades with the rector.

When the truth came out and Donald realised who had betrayed and willingly sacrificed his friends for her own feelings, he settled his heart on bachelordom. Lizzie, at least, would never be his bride. Their already tempestuous courtship seemed shipwrecked beyond rescue. How then was it that they were now many months married and happily promenading on the stone harbour wall this very morning? Donald, of course, had been implicated deeply in the smuggling adventures. He was then, and is now, very closely wrapped up in friendship with their leader, the worthy Rector of Lower Penzle. The rector, true to his pastoral responsibilities, had followed the events of Donald's courtship and had guided them back into open waters after what seemed to them both to be the total wrecking of their friendship. It was a happy day when bells rang out and a church filled with villagers watched the young couple joined in matrimony. The rector, ever a perfectionist regarding his comments at weddings, excelled himself as he expostulated on the saying that 'true love never runs smooth'. But from the day of their marriage the waters had run smooth and sunlit for them both, and they often remarked that they might have missed their married bliss had they not had the wise counsel of the rector. Indeed, their counsellor had even made Captain Williams seem the very reason for their marriage, but this they had never communicated to the officer of the Crown in retirement.

This morning was the first time the three had come face-to-face in such close proximity. The Captain eased himself from one side to the other in discomfort and embarrassment, but the young couple walked to within a few feet of him and sat down without so much as a look in his direction. They were engrossed in conversation. The Captain eyed them out of the corner of his eye and wished he had the ability of a chameleon to melt into the stonework – at least in colour. In a moment his bright-red face, blushing with increasing embarrassment, would have changed him back into an all-too-obvious spectacle, for there, before his sidewards gaze, the two had swept into each other's embrace. They stayed that way till a little nervous cough from their observer made them aware that they were not alone.

"Oh, Captain Williams, sir, you must be the first to know our news."

"Ahem, ma'm, I am delighted to see you both this fine morning. And, what might your special intelligence be for an officer of the Crown, ma'm?" His manner was as formal as if he were back on duty, but it was missed by the young woman as she looked first at her husband and then at the Captain.

"We are going to have a baby, sir. That is our news, and you are the first one to know in the whole of Lower Penzle."

Captain Willoughby Winton Williams rose and bowed low before the mother-to-be.

"Ma'm, young sir, I am honoured to be such an early recipient of such glorious news. May I congratulate you both and wish you a fine son, or daughter – or maybe both!"

"Oh, sir, I hope you are not prophetical in such a wish, for Donald and I would have a hard job to feed two young mouths on Donald's little salary at the draper's establishment. But I appreciate your kind wishes and thank you."

"And I would like to say something to you, Captain, if I may," added Donald. "I have not seen you since the happening of last year which put us at odds. If you will allow me to say so, I do not hold anything against you, good sir. I accept that you were doing your duty, and, whilst I did not take kindly to your using Lizzie here, the rector showed us both that but for that night we should not have ended the racket. We would still be forced to continue our efforts, and that would mean that Lizzie here and I would never have been married. So maybe, sir, we owe it to you that we are this morning rejoicing in the news we share with you."

The Captain was dumfounded into silence. He coughed, cleared his throat, and made as though he would deliver a speech, but when he opened his mouth a most ridiculous squeak came out. Donald and Lizzie giggled, to the embarrassment of them all. The Captain stepped forward and, with his usual theatrical manner, gripped both of their arms in his chubby hands.

"My dears, I have today resolved to put many things behind me that I am not proud of. You have helped me to feel a bigger man. I thank you both for this moment of joy, and I go on my way to do something I had resolved to do but could not find strength to do. Thank you!"

With that said, the Captain bowed and left them. He hurried back along the harbour wall and up the hill towards the rectory. Donald and Lizzie watched him go.

Donald turned to Lizzie and took her again into his arms. "I must get back to the shop, Liz," he said. "But before I do, let me make a crazy suggestion to you."

"Everything is a bit crazy this morning, Donald. What now, my love?"

"I suggest that we ask Captain Williams to be the godfather to our child!"

CHAPTER FIFTEEN

Mrs Jones' Humble Pie

Mrs Jones had just taken a large pie from the oven when the bell of the rectory door rang loudly. This astute housekeeper seemed to know who was holding on to the bell pull. She hurriedly covered the steaming pie with a cloth and placed it on the cold slab of the pantry shelf. The bell rang again, and she called as she bustled along the hallway, "I'm coming! I'm coming!"

She wiped her hands on her apron and opened the door.

"Ma'm, I am sorry if I appeared impatient. I do apologise. Is the rector at home?"

"No, Captain, he is not. I accept your apology, but tell me: how is it that you always know when I am baking a special pie? I somehow knew it was you at the door, for I was just then taking my pie out of the oven."

"Ma'm, nothing was further from my mind than your delicious pies – but now you mention it, I can smell that pastry from here."

"Well, don't stand there – come in and wait. The rector will be in for lunch soon.

The smell that pervaded the hallway overcame Captain Williams' politeness, and he stumbled after Mrs Jones when normally he would have either waited in the hall or entered the small sitting room to his left. He stood in the kitchen doorway and hurriedly whisked his large handkerchief to his chin to catch the dribble of saliva that trickled from one corner of his mouth.

He regained his composure, however, and after an introductory cough boldly announced his news to a bewildered Mrs Jones: "Ma'm, we are about to have a baby!"

A stunned Mrs Jones clasped her hands together and withdrew into the corner of her kitchen.

"Captain Williams, sir, have you been drinking?"

"No, ma'm, I think you misunderstand me."

"I most certainly do, sir. I am a respectable widow of many years, and you have always behaved as a perfect gentleman, yet you step into my kitchen and tell me that *we* are to have a baby. Perhaps you would be good enough to tell me just what this is all about?"

"Ma'm, it is perfectly simple: what I am telling you is that the parish council is going to have a baby!"

"Now, Captain Williams, I believe you have taken leave of your senses."

Before the Captain could exonerate himself, the door opened from the backyard and the rector stood there, filling its tall framework.

"Well, well, Captain Williams, I am glad to see you. Have you heard the good news, sir? We are going to have a baby!"

Mrs Jones let out a little scream and sat down hurriedly in her high-backed wooden armchair.

"Mrs Jones, are you all right?"

"No, sir, I am not! And if anyone else comes into my kitchen and tells me that they, or we, are going to have a baby, I shall believe I am housekeeper to a madhouse and not Lower Penzle Rectory."

"Ho ho! So we already have the news, do we? I thought I was the first to be told. Mrs Jones, this morning Lizzie Creedy has announced to her husband that she is to present him with a baby in a few months' time."

"Well then, why didn't somebody tell me?" asked Mrs Jones with a smile fit to crack her face. "First Captain Williams has a baby, and then you, sir, have one. At least I can understand when you tell me that Lizzie Slocum is to have one."

"Mrs Jones, Lizzie has been Mrs Creedy these many months, so this was to be hoped for. Now we can rejoice with them. Captain Williams, will you kindly join us for dinner?"

The Captain, who had been sitting in a corner chair waiting for the air of mystery to clear, was now suddenly revived. He drew himself up to his full military height and accepted, with due restraint, this kind offer of celebration.

As the meal progressed from celery soup to beefsteak pie, carrots, peas, new potatoes, rich gravy, all with second helpings, the conversation was somewhat limited; but then the rector turned to Captain Williams and suggested that there might have been a reason for his visit to the rectory.

"Indeed there is, sir." The Captain dabbed his chin, absent-mindedly put more into his mouth, and explained: "These past days have set me thinking, sir, and I don't like what I have been thinking. I have come to ask your pardon, sir."

"My dear Captain, I am not in the habit of taking confessions. Such does not fit my churchmanship. Tell me what it is that I must pardon you for. If you are thinking of matters connected with your military duty, there is no pardon required. I have told you before: you did your duty by His Majesty, and I have no quarrel with that, sir."

"Oh no, good sir, I hold no sense of guilt in that case, except that I took so long to uncover your plot and apprehend your person. No, I am sure we can both look back on those days without regret. No, I refer to something much more recent, and I eat this day a larger slice of humble pie than I do of Mrs Jones' delicious beefsteak pie. Excellent, ma'm! Excellent!"

Mrs Jones reached a hand out for the Captain's plate, and the rector smiled at both of them as he hesitated not a moment in handing it over for more of the same.

"Good sir, I have been a fool – an arrogant, pompous fool! You have guessed, I am sure, that Monsieur Latreque employed me to watch you and trap you whenever I could. I thought myself clever enough to outwit you, sir. I even thought myself right in trying to. But I have been thinking, sir, and I don't like what I have been thinking. Monsieur Latreque has shown me more of the ways of his revolution than I care to be associated with. To think of it! I offered for a guinea or two to hinder your efforts to rescue men and women from a wretched system that condemns men without a proper trial and hopes somehow to bring about a new day. No, sir, I do not like what I have been thinking, and I come to ask your pardon for my arrogant pride in thinking that I was someone special, working for a righteous cause. I am ashamed of myself! I am ashamed of myself!"

The rector noted that despite all the contrition of this little military man he never for a moment forgot where his mouth was.

"My dear Captain, we have seen some battles together and found ourselves, twice over, fighting on the right side. I give you my hand and take you at your word. I believe you really have seen the light of day in this matter. You are a respected member of our village community. I trust the future will see our friendship become a strong and lasting one. Mrs Jones, is there any more of your delicious 'humble' pie? I do believe I will join the Captain in a little more."

The Captain ate humble pie and enjoyed every bit of it.

"Oh, by the way, Captain Williams, I understand from the Creedys that you are to be asked to stand as godfather for this addition to their family!"

"I am? Well, then I treat this meal as a celebration, sir. Today I have made my peace with the village of Lower Penzle. There doesn't happen to be just a small piece of that pie left with which to celebrate, does there?"

CHAPTER SIXTEEN

Mrs Jones Is All at Sea

The *Sea Winkle* had come and gone many times with no news of Jack Dart, nor of Latreque. The rector carried on his round of clerical activities with his usual thoroughness. Parish council meetings often discussed the happenings and watched carefully for signs of needed help from across the Channel. When the next cry for help came, it happened that the rector was out of town. His visit to London kept him away for two whole weeks, and Joseph Trenbeath met with the parish men in the rector's study, not expecting anything earth-shattering to take place.

Jack Dart appeared, much as he had done on the first occasion they had all met. The council meeting was almost over when Mrs Jones announced his presence, and all stood at his entrance in respect and greeting. When he heard of the rector's absence, Jack showed signs of dejection. He surveyed the group and made his plea. A young man had escaped only an hour before his head was to fall beneath the guillotine. He now lay in hiding in a French port, and Jack had come to ask the rector to help get him across the Channel. Every day his danger increased as soldiers searched the ports.

Mrs Jones entered with a hot drink for all present, and she overheard the gloomy comments that issued from Joseph.

"If I were a young man and had the courage of the rector, I would do something myself," he said. "Is there no chance that we can await the rector's return?"

"I fear not, Monsieur. If we do not act this week, all is lost. No man can easily escape from Latreque in his present mood. He hunts with the fury of a lion these days."

Mrs Jones whispered to Joseph, and the old chairman gasped and shook his head.

Mrs Jones would not accept his negative attitude, so, as she collected Jack Dart's cup, she whispered to him that she had something to say to him in private. Jack quietly left the room behind the housekeeper and they remained for some minutes outside the door. When he came back he said nothing to the company but accepted their apologies for their inability to help him in the absence of their leader.

The time came for the meeting to be dismissed, and only Jack remained in the rector's study. Mrs Jones came in and sat down – a thing she rarely did in this sanctum of the master of the house.

"Well, what do you think?" she asked as she looked into Jack Dart's eyes.

"Madame, I never cease to wonder at you English. First I discover your wonderful rector, and now I hear you saying that you, a frail old woman, would risk your life in the cause of my people."

"I am not English, sir, but Welsh, and I don't think I would have survived in this household if I had been a frail old woman. I am willing to do my part. The rector has risked his life more than once, from what I hear, and I stand right with him and yourself, sir, in what you are doing. I cannot see why I cannot take dishes to France as well as the rector, and I'm sure I will make as good a lady as he does."

"Madame, I am honoured to know you!" Jack Dart rose and bowed. "I shall let you know the time of the next sailing of the *Sea Winkle*. Now I must leave. Goodnight, and thank you!"

The door closed and Mrs Jones ran upstairs to the little bedroom, where she tried on one black dress after another.

All were too long. She would have to get busy with needle and thread. She took the lamp up as the kitchen clock struck one. As she climbed the stairs to her room, she chuckled to herself.

"You must have taken leave of your senses," she whispered as she set her lamp on the wash-hand stand.

She slept well, but dreamed of being chased and tripping on the hem of her long black dress.

Two days later a young lad brought her a note from Jack Dart. She was to meet him at the Terrapin Inn on the harbourside at Crendon Bywater.

When she arrived on Timothy Wiseman's cart, she had help to carry her large basket into the inn and up the stairs to Jack Dart's room. His answer to her knock told her he was nervous. She entered and had the large basket placed in the centre of the room; Jack greeted her warmly and bade her sit down.

"May I order some refreshment for you, Madame?"

"No, thank you, Mr Dart. I am anxious that I get into my dress. If you would be kind enough to leave the room, I will be ready in two shakes of a dog's tail."

"Madame, there are no dogs here, but I will leave you to shake its tail just the same."

Mrs Jones locked the door. Hurriedly she unclasped the basket and took out the heavy black dress. She placed it over her own clothing, and the transformation was striking. Not only did she now look fatter, but she looked decidedly severe in this dress and hooded bonnet. She unlocked the door, and Jack Dart whistled as he surveyed his new companion.

"But, Madame, I would not recognise you."

"That's what I hoped, Mr Dart. I hope no one else will either. Come now – into the basket with you. Oh, let me remove my dishes first."

The *Sea Winkle* sailed on the morning tide, and, apart from one or two uneasy moments as she waited for her stomach to find her sea legs, Mrs Jones began to enjoy this adventure.

At the port of disembarkation it was a different matter. Latreque was in his coach at the quayside. Mrs Jones spotted him and held back from having her precious basket unloaded. When it was unloaded, Latreque had his men follow the lady into the warehouse; and there, hiding in the shadows, they awaited the expected transformation. When Mrs Jones sat on the basket, whispering as she did to Jack Dart within that there was danger in the air, Latreque himself approached.

"Good day, Madame!" he said with mock politeness, but before she could answer he reached for her hood and pulled it off her head. His shocked gasp at the sight of Mrs Jones' grey hair drawn back in her usual bun, neatly pinned, gave her great satisfaction. Latreque spluttered in his consternation and proffered his apology. It did not dawn upon him that Mrs Jones should not have been in France. He bowed to her, apologised again, and cursed as he called his men to follow him out of the warehouse.

Jack Dart was out of the basket and away in the shadows before Latreque could change his mind and come back. He was only just in time, for, although Latreque himself did not appear, his men came back to offer mocking assistance to a lady with a heavy load. They picked up her basket, in spite of her protestations, and loaded it on to a Paris-bound coach.

She climbed aboard and was duly set down outside Notre Dame Cathedral. She looked around her in dismay. What now would she do, a stranger in this great city? She had visions of her head being severed from her shoulders. But when she was about to sit again on her basket, this time in sheer exhaustion, another set of hands lifted it and quietly bade her follow.

She found herself descending steps into the crypt of the great cathedral, and in a moment she was embraced by Jack Dart himself.

"Madame Jones, you are the bravest old woman I know."

"Not so much of the old, if you don't mind! I may feel it just now, but I do not like to admit it at any time, Mr Dart."

The next day, Mrs Jones, her precious basket and her deep-hooded cloak were again on the deck of the *Sea Winkle*. Latreque watched her go on board, too confused and embarrassed by his previous disrobing effort to touch the old woman from England as she safely escorted her basketed escapee under the very nose of his enemies. The rector would have been proud of his housekeeper for more than her cooking had he seen her wave to Latreque as the ship sailed out from the French quay. Mrs Jones was all at sea indeed!

CHAPTER SEVENTEEN

As We Forgive Those Who Trespass Against Us

Pierre Latreque stood visibly trembling outside his own courtroom. How many times he had presided at the People's Court he could not remember, but today it was he who was to be judged. The tide of the revolution was ebbing, and the zealots were looking for further heads to roll. In his ardour for the cause, Pierre had persecuted any who dared speak against the regime. Finally, when his own wife had made it known that she could no longer uphold the rigours of the Revolutionary Council and watch her own friends being taken to the Bastille and the guillotine, Pierre had tried to shield her from discovery. His love for his wife was to cost him dear. When her views were made public, she was immediately incarcerated, and he was arrested for supporting her views. His denial was useless. He knew all too well that they would not listen to him, as he had not listened to others. He had bred a brood of serpents, and they were now to bite the hand that had fed them.

He entered the room as his name was called, and he heard the charges against himself and his wife. No chance was given for defence. There was no opportunity to explain or repent. He heard his sentence: he, with his wife, was to face death by the end of the month. Fifteen days of life! He thought at that moment of all those he had condemned in that room, and knew only despair.

News travelled fast, and, as on so many other days, the vaults of Notre Dame heard the quiet tones of Jack Dart reading the names of those who had been condemned at that day's court. When Pierre and Marie Latreque's names were read, even Jack found it hard to refrain from a comment. Here was his arch-enemy within the very prison to which he had consigned his brother.

It happened that this was one of the rare occasions when the rector was paying a visit to the Continent. He too was there to hear the unbelievable news. Jack came to where the rector stood in the shadows.

"What does my English friend think now of this revolution which feeds off its own kind? It is eating itself to destruction, and the sooner it has satisfied itself the better. There will yet be peace and sanity in our beloved land."

"Yes, Jack, my friend, I suppose this is what some would call poetic justice. The hunter has been hunted. But, Jack, what of the plans for your brother's release?"

"I fear we are no nearer finding a way to extricate him. His illness is worse, I hear, according to the nuns who have been within that stinking prison cell."

"Did you say nuns are allowed into his cell?" asked the rector with excitement in his voice. "Then I have an idea, Jack."

And so it was that some two days later two nuns from a convent under the jurisdiction of the Bishop of Notre Dame made their way to the great gates of the Bastille. The nuns were well known, and they were admitted with some sarcasm by the prison authorities. Religion was at a low ebb in France, and such servants of the church were tolerated rather than appreciated.

The two elderly Sisters of Mercy made their way from one cell to another. Most prisoners were chained or crowded into dormitory-like stone cells, where they stood or sat in groups. Younger, more active prisoners talked; older, long-term inmates simply sat and stared. The whole atmosphere was one of hopelessness. No one escaped the notice of the guard, who stood on a raised platform and surveyed the motley crowd and now and again shouted abuse or some ribald comment at an aristocratic nobleman or dainty young gentlewoman.

The nuns passed on their way and finally came to a cell with just two prisoners sitting on either side of a rough wooden table. They were not holding a conversation. When the nuns were admitted by the guard, the younger of the two men tried to stand, but he had great difficulty. He showed signs of weakness, but offered his chair to the women. The other man – much older – was none other than Pierre Latreque. He looked up as the women entered, but he did not rise. Antoine Dart, the younger man, rebuked him and shamefacedly Latreque stood and bowed. His face showed signs of lack of sleep and his hair had not been combed. The young man asked after his relatives and the nuns handed him a note. He read and reread it. Then he took a long look at the two women and passed the note to Latreque.

Latreque read the note and almost blurted out an exclamation, but the younger man held his finger to his lips and Latreque controlled himself. Without another word, the nuns began to undress. The men turned aside, but they were quickly turned back by the older of the two nuns, who urged them to put on the clothing. The nuns had stripped off their outer habits, yet they were still dressed as before. They had been wearing a second habit. A moment later the men, too, appeared to be two very striking nuns.

The door of the cell had been left unlocked, and one of the men stood close to it and looked along the long vaulted hallway. The guard was away at the other end. The four nuns left the cell and walked in opposite directions – the women to continue their rounds, and the disguised men to make their way to the main gates. Each step was a trial to the younger man. His extreme weakness made him lurch and stumble many times. The older man, who had not shown a single thought of concern for his companion before now, steadied him and spoke words of encouragement. They had to go only a few hundred yards, but it seemed to them both like a journey of a hundred miles. Each guard seemed, to their imaginations, to be staring at their faces. Both had been shaved by the prison barber that morning, so there were no whiskers to betray them, and their stiff, white hoods hid their facial contours.

Finally the gate was reached. The fear was that as soon as they spoke they would be recognised.

Suddenly a loud explosion was heard in the street. The guard on duty rushed to the gate and spied through the grill. A carriage was hurrying away, and in the road were the remains of a small powder keg. The guard was so busy eyeing the scene that he hardly noticed the nuns. He swung open the small wicket gate and they stepped into the sunlight and hurried on their way towards Notre Dame. Another explosion attracted the guard's attention, and he closed the gate and lifted the heavy bar into place. Something was happening out there which could threaten the security of the prison, and he was determined not to lose his head by allowing an escape!

An hour later, two more nuns approached the outer gate and were challenged by a senior guard. Two nuns had already passed out of the gate, so who were these two? Only two nuns had been recorded as entering the prison that day, so these were obviously two escapees. They were roughly pushed into a gatehouse room, and, before they could remonstrate, they were stripped of their habits. They sang out their fearful protests, and it was not long before their clean underclothing and well-fed bodies made it all too clear that the guards were mistaken. Not given to apologies, they left the nuns to dress again and let them go. The question was now asked, who were the first two nuns?

Shortly afterwards the cry went out from the cell: "Latreque and Dart have escaped! Heads will roll for this."

A pair of horsemen galloped out from the gates of the Bastille, but by nightfall no trace had been found of the two escapees. Actually, they mingled among the scanty worshippers at the cathedral evensong, and, dressed now as Parisienne housewives, they walked slowly to a house at the side of the river. A tall woman joined them as they entered, and she whispered in perfect French, if a little deeper than one would expect from a female, that she trusted they would sleep well and be ready before dawn for a journey by barge down the river.

That night, now a free man, Pierre Latreque asked Antoine Dart his first civil question since they had been put together in a cell – one a supporter of the regime, but condemned by it to death; the other a fighter against all that the revolution stood for, paying for his stand by long years of incarceration. Both had now been freed by the same simple, yet daring, plan.

"Who", asked Latreque, "do we thank for our escape? Do you have any idea, Dart, who would succour a man with my past and open the door of the Bastille for such a queer pair of cell mates as us?"

Before the younger man could answer, the tall woman entered, and, swinging off her cloak, spoke in perfect English: "Pierre, Antoine, allow me to answer that question. Two very brave ladies of the church nearly paid dearly for your release this afternoon. But our prayers were answered, and with a little explosion or two we were able to make sure you were well clear. They too are safe. Now you are my guests, and in a couple of days, God helping us, we shall be safely in England's green and pleasant land."

Pierre Latreque could not believe his eyes. There sat the Rector of Lower Penzle. This man whom he viewed as his enemy, whom he suspected of complicity in more than one escape, and from whom he had expected not a sympathetic thought had been involved in some way in bringing about his escape.

On the *Sea Winkle*, some days later, Pierre Latreque eased himself from a large basket from which the lady in black had removed her dishes and sat looking down at his feet.

The rector opened the conversation: "Pierre, my friend, you were nearly the victim of that wonderful France you have boasted of. You have lost your beloved wife to the guillotine and almost lost your own head there too. I trust you will accept my invitation to stay at the rectory for a few days to renew your strength before deciding what you will do with your life now."

"My dear rector, I do not know what to say. I am humbled to the dust by what has happened. Why would you help a man like me to escape? Surely you cannot forgive me for what you know I and my so-called new France have done?"

The change in his voice was like spring after a hard winter.

The rector answered by opening his small prayer book and reading softly from the Lord's Prayer: "Forgive us our trespasses as we forgive those who trespass against us."

Latreque turned his eyes away, and through his tears he caught the first sight of England.